MIDNIGHT PHONE CALLS

Book created by A. E. Parker

Written by Eric Weiner

Based on characters from the Parker Brothers® game

A Creative Media Applications Production

SCHOLASTIC INC.
New York Toronto London Auckland Sydney

Special thanks to: Diane Morris, Sandy Upham, Susan Nash, Laura Millhollin, Chris Lataille, Liz Sheppard, Jean Feiwel, Greg Holch, Dona Smith, Nancy Smith, John Simko, and Elizabeth Parisi

ISBN 0-590-47804-4

12 11 10 9 8 7 6 5 4 3 4 5 6 7 8 9/9

Printed in the U.S.A. 40

First Scholastic printing, April 1994

MIDNIGHT PHONE CALLS

Look for these books in the
Clue™ series:

#1 WHO KILLED MR. BODDY?
#2 THE *SECRET* SECRET PASSAGE
#3 THE CASE OF THE INVISIBLE CAT
#4 MYSTERY AT THE MASKED BALL
#5 MIDNIGHT PHONE CALLS

For Jacob, Joshua, Hana Rose, Danny,
Ahava, Claire, Aviva, Harvey, Arielle, Tobias,
and Atara

Contents

MIDNIGHT PHONE CALLS

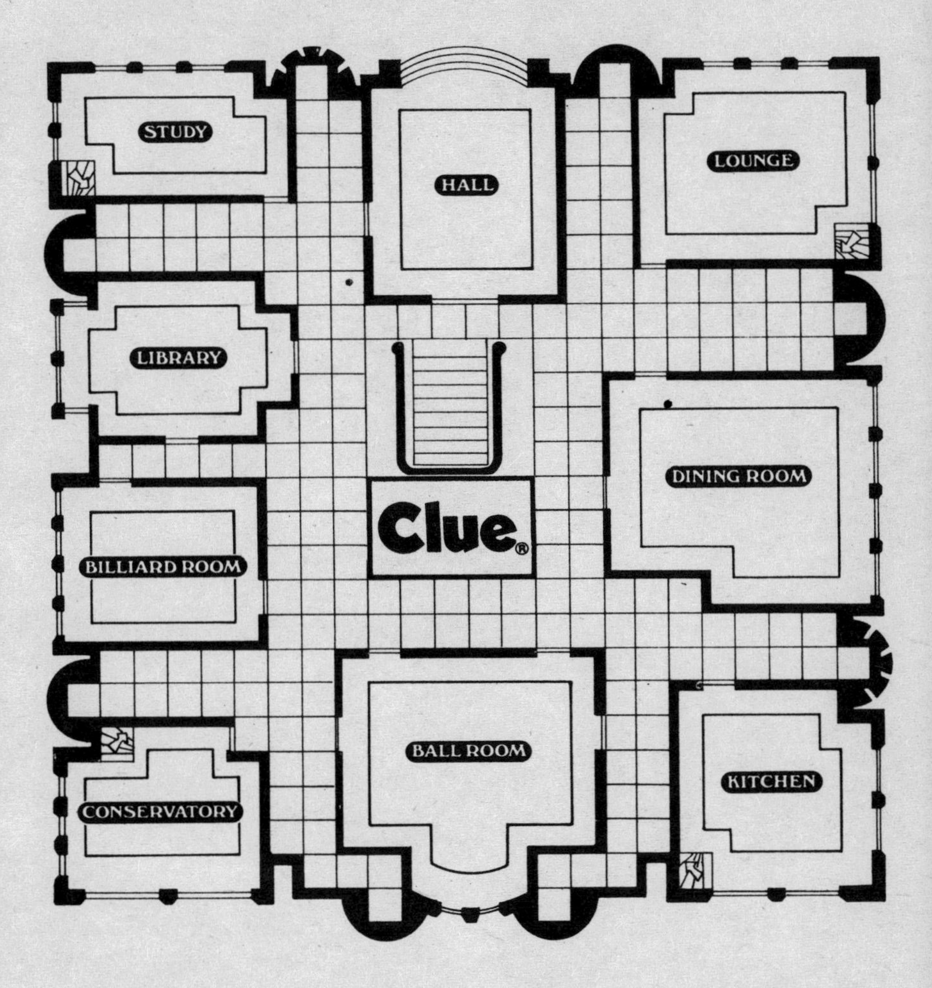
STUDY
HALL
LOUNGE
LIBRARY
DINING ROOM
Clue®
BILLIARD ROOM
BALL ROOM
KITCHEN
CONSERVATORY

Allow Me to Introduce Myself . . .

MY NAME IS REGINALD BODDY, AND I have the honor of being your host at the mansion this weekend. My other guests? Oh, they'll be arriving soon in the Boddy private jet.

Too soon.

You see, my other guests are a real bunch of jokesters. For instance, you may recall that the last time you dropped by, Colonel Mustard shot and killed me. Well, it turned out that Mustard hadn't used a real Revolver at all. It was just a starter pistol he used to signal the beginning of races. When he realized his mistake, he got a real Revolver and fired *that* at me. But, of course, he missed. Ha-ha, what a kidder!

Er . . . would you mind shutting the Study door just a sec? Can you still hear me when I *whisper* like this? I've got a favor to ask. I want you to keep an eye on the other guests for me. Not that a horrible accident or crime will occur this time! *But* . . . if it does, and you keep your eyes peeled, you can tell me whodunit, all right?

You have only six suspects to watch. (I, myself,

will never be a suspect, of course!) The six suspects are :

Miss Scarlet: Few people know that this stunning beauty has a heart of gold. She likes to keep it a secret since she stole that heart from a jewelry shop!

Professor Plum: Please remember to say hello to Professor Plum. He's a bit forgetful, you see, and he likes to be reminded of his own name.

Mrs. Peacock: A delightful woman, but just a bit on the prim and proper side. For instance, I once burped in her presence, and she called the police.

Mr. Green: I was telling Mr. Green just yesterday that he's a bit of a bully. But he threatened to pinch me if I didn't take it back. Suddenly I realized he's not a bully at all!

Colonel Mustard: A gallant and noble man. But you might say he has a *duel* personality. He's always challenging everyone to a duel. Well, at least there's never a *duel* moment!

Mrs. White: My sweet, loyal maid always wears a smile. Hmm . . . I do wish she'd take that smile-mask off so I could see how she's really feeling!

To help you in your detective work, I'll provide a list of all the possible suspects, weapons, and rooms at the end of each mystery. As you read, you can check off suspects until you've narrowed your list down to one.

Speaking of suspects, the other guests should be arriving any minute now. In fact, I think I just heard the Boddy jet crashing into the Conservatory.

Crashing into the Conservatory?!

Er . . . will you excuse me?

1
Party Crashers

EEEEEEEEEEEEEEEEEEEEEEEEEE-
OOOOOOOOOOOOOOOOOOOOOOOOOOOO-
WWWWWWWWWWWWWWWWW!!!!!!!!!!!!!!

The silver plane screamed through the air, hurtling straight down . . . down . . . down. . . .

Oh, no! The Boddy jet was heading right toward the Boddy mansion! Unless the pilot could regain control of the plane it would —
CRASSSSSSSSSSSSHHHHHHHHHHHHHH!!!!!

The jet smashed right through the Conservatory window.

And then, for a moment, all was silent.

The mansion's front doors flew open. Out ran the little billionaire himself, Mr. Boddy. He was followed by his faithful maid, Mrs. White. She was clutching the brass Candlestick, which she'd been in the middle of polishing when the plane crashed.

Sure enough, the jet's silver tail was sticking straight out of the mansion. Black smoke billowed everywhere. Mr. Boddy gaped at the accident in horror. Mrs. White did the same. Then she turned her back and grinned.

"Oh, Mrs. White!" Mr. Boddy clutched his maid's arm. "The guests — they were all on that plane!"

"Don't worry, they still are," Mrs. White said dryly.

Mr. Boddy's knees knocked together. He clutched his bald head with both hands. "But . . . but . . . they're all dead!"

Mrs. White lifted her eyes to heaven in silent prayer and whispered one word: "*Yes!*"

But while she was looking up at the sky, she saw —

What was it? It looked like no more than a dot.

A *purple* dot.

Whatever the dot was, it was getting bigger and bigger. "Look!" she cried, pointing with the Candlestick.

Mr. Boddy appeared confused. "You polished the Candlestick beautifully," he said. "But I've got more important things on my mind."

"No," she said, pointing again. "Look — *there*!"

Now Boddy saw it, too. It was a huge purple parachute, gliding slowly to the ground.

Hanging from the parachute was a tall man in

a purple cardigan sweater and a leather aviator helmet. In one hand he held a silver Wrench. He appeared to be lost in thought. He was taken totally by surprise when he hit the ground.

Boddy and White ran forward yelling, "Professor Plum!"

"What?" Plum asked from underneath the purple parchute.

Mr. Boddy and Mrs. White yanked away the parachute. Professor Plum's face lit up when he saw his host. "Mr. Boddy," he said. "Great to see you! Where's the party?"

"There's no party!" Mr. Boddy cried impatiently. "Tell me what happened. What caused the accident?"

Plum stared at Mr. Boddy long and hard. Finally he asked, "What accident?"

It was clear that the forgetful professor wasn't going to be able to shed much light on the plane crash.

But just then Mrs. White spotted another parachute floating down. This parachute was scarlet, and so was the parachutist.

The gorgeous Miss Scarlet was holding onto the parachute with only one hand. In her other hand she twirled the Revolver. She landed gracefully despite her high-heel shoes. Then she yanked off her aviator cap, and shook her long mane of jet-black hair.

"Reginald, darling!" she called cheerfully as she stalked across the lawn toward her host. "Plum told us you were having a party."

"That's a mistake," Boddy said, blushing bright red. "Oh, I'm so relieved. You're okay!"

"I'm *okay*?" Miss Scarlet tickled Boddy's nose with her red boa. "Surely you think I'm better than *that*?"

"But how did you survive?" Mrs. White asked glumly.

"Well don't sound so disappointed," Miss Scarlet said with a laugh. Then she explained what had happened. "Colonel Mustard was flying the plane," she said. "Mr. Green wanted to pilot, but Mustard wouldn't let him. He kept reminding Mr. Green about the time he drove Mr. Boddy's golf cart right through the — "

"Oh, please, don't remind *me*," Mr. Boddy said quickly. "It was only yesterday that the workmen finished repairing the wall to the Billiard Room."

Miss Scarlet giggled. "Well, anyway, Mustard kept teasing Mr. Green until finally Green clonked Mustard on the head with the Lead Pipe, and the plane went into a nosedive. Everyone else is dead."

"Everyone?" Plum asked, looking confused.

"Except for you," Scarlet told him.

"Ah," Plum said, looking relieved.

Which is when plump Mrs. Peacock landed on his head.

She had parachuted right down on top of him, knocking him to the ground. For a moment, Mrs. Peacock and Plum both thrashed around wildly under the peacock-blue parachute. Then a Knife slashed a hole in the blue cloth, and Mrs. Peacock popped out. She was wearing a leather aviator helmet, with her peacock feather stuck on top. She was holding the Knife.

"I heard what you were saying about the accident," Mrs. Peacock told Miss Scarlet. "I must say, it's very rude to lie. Plum was driving the plane, and Miss Scarlet here bonked him with the Lead Pipe."

"Ha!" Miss Scarlet scoffed. "Nonsense!"

"You *disagree*?!" Mrs. Peacock drew herself up straight. "How impertinent of you! How vulgar!"

Plum had made his way out from the blue parachute and was tenderly stroking his head. "Miss Scarlet hit me?" he asked. "No wonder I can't remember."

"You can never remember," Mrs. White reminded him.

"That's right," Plum recalled. "I forgot." He

kept rubbing his head. "But I still feel like I've got a headache. Refresh my memory. Did someone just land on my head?"

Mrs. Peacock rolled her eyes. "Anyway," she told Mr. Boddy, "that's what *really* happened. Believe me. Now, when does the party start?"

"But I'm not having a party right now," Mr. Boddy told her.

"Why, how rude!" Miss Peacock said huffily. Just then, a green parachute settled onto the front lawn. Mr. Green was underneath, with the Rope.

"Don't listen to any of them," Mr. Green snarled. "I'll tell you all what *really* happened. *I* was piloting the plane. Mustard got jealous, because Miss Scarlet wanted to sit next to me in the cockpit."

"You're dreaming, Mr. Green," purred Miss Scarlet. "But maybe I'll sit next to you at the party."

"There is no party!" Mr. Boddy snapped.

Mr. Green ignored them both. "Then Mustard challenged me to a duel," he went on, "and he bonked me on the head with the Lead Pipe. That's why we crashed. And if anyone disagrees with me . . ." Mr. Green made a scary face and threatened, "I'll tickle you silly!"

"I disagree!" shouted Colonel Mustard.

All the guests looked straight up.

Here came Colonel Mustard, floating down under a mustard-yellow parachute. He was just a few feet over their heads. "I've never heard such lies in all my life," he roared. "I challenge you all to a duel!"

"A duel? Oh, not now," Boddy begged. "I think we've had enough excitement for one day, don't you?"

"But *I* was piloting the plane," Mustard insisted. "That's why I'm the last to arrive. I hope I'm not too late for the party."

Mr. Boddy stamped his foot in frustration.

"You certainly are taking your sweet time about getting here," Plum remarked. For Mustard was still floating a few yards overhead.

"I'm stuck in the tree, you ninny!" cried Mustard.

"Hmmm," Boddy said, scratching his bald head. "So many different stories. You all must be so shook up from the accident that you're not clearly remembering what happened. He looked at his guests. "One of you must remember correctly. But who?"

"Me!" insisted all five of his guests at once.

Boddy kept thinking. "Let's see. I know that only five of the mansion's six weapons were on the flight . . ."

Suddenly Plum shouted, "I REMEMBER!"

Everyone looked at him, waiting for the professor's great insight.

"Um, I left my purple luggage on the plane," Plum explained.

WHO ATTACKED THE PILOT OF THE PLANE?

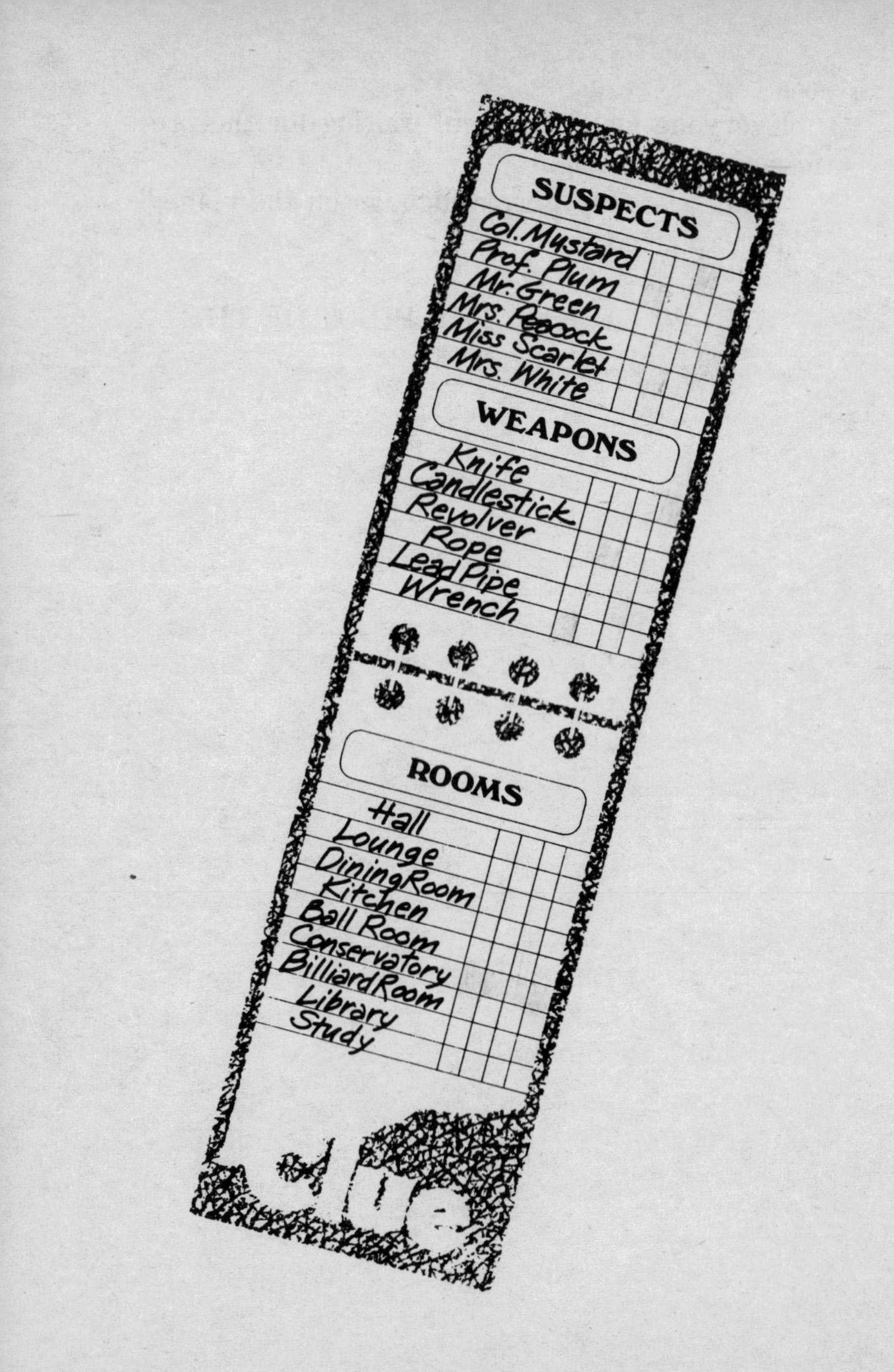
SUSPECTS
Col. Mustard
Prof. Plum
Mr. Green
Mrs. Peacock
Miss Scarlet
Mrs. White
WEAPONS
Knife
Candlestick
Revolver
Rope
Lead Pipe
Wrench
ROOMS
Hall
Lounge
Dining Room
Kitchen
Ball Room
Conservatory
Billiard Room
Library
Study

13

SOLUTION

COLONEL MUSTARD with the LEAD PIPE

By the process of elimination, we know that Colonel Mustard had the Lead Pipe. That means, only Mr. Green's story holds up. For instance, Miss Scarlet said that Mr. Green had the Lead Pipe, but Green is carrying the Rope.

Luckily for the Colonel, everyone was in such shock from the accident that, by the next morning, no one could remember a thing about what had happened. Mr. Boddy was glad they also forgot that they had thought he was giving a party. In fact, he was so happy, he's started thinking of having a party — to celebrate!

2
Midnight Phone Calls

OUTSIDE THE MANSION, THE NIGHT WAS cold, rainy, and dark. But inside the Library, the guests were all warm and cozy.

"Ah, literature, literature," sighed Colonel Mustard. Like the other guests, he had his nose buried in one of the many fine titles in Boddy's excellent collection of comic books.

Only one guest wasn't reading — Miss Scarlet. She stared out the window, into the rain, into the darkness.

Just then, something tapped against the glass, making Miss Scarlet shriek.

All the guests looked up at her, startled.

"Just the branch of a tree," Miss Scarlet explained, blushing as red as her name. She turned quickly from the window.

Too quickly. She stubbed her toe against the leg of the Library's main reading table. "Ow!" she cried, hopping around the room in pain.

"You're awfully jumpy tonight, aren't you, Miss Scarlet?" observed Mr. Green, his eyes narrowing with suspicion. "What's up?"

"Oh, nothing," Miss Scarlet insisted. "Nothing at all."

The guests returned to their comic books, but every few seconds, they all lowered them an inch, to spy on Miss Scarlet. When she caught them looking, they quickly raised the comic books back in front of their faces.

"I don't trust that woman," muttered Green behind his comic book.

Mustard promptly lowered his comic book and slapped Green in the face with a yellow glove. "Insulting Miss Scarlet, eh?" he roared. "I challenge you to a duel!"

As the two men began counting off their paces, Miss Scarlet glanced at her watch. Almost midnight. She tiptoed toward the door. "Please, don't mind me," she said. "I'm fine. And if you will all excuse me, I have to make a . . . *private* phone call."

No one seemed to be listening. *So much the better*, she thought. She slid the Library door shut behind her. From inside, she began hearing screams, crashes, and gunshots as Mustard and Green fought their duel. Now was the perfect time. Now she would not be disturbed.

She hurried through the mansion to the Dining Room. After locking both Dining Room doors, she glanced at her watch again. The minute hand moved. It now pointed straight up to twelve. She picked up the phone and placed her call.

In a hushed voice, she asked, "Well? Did you get my jewels?" She listened for a moment, then purred, "Excellent!"

Just then, Mr. Green slid open the Library door. "I'm tired of dueling with you, Mustard," he growled. "I'm going to bed!"

In response, a Knife came flying out at Green. He ducked. The Knife stuck into the wall behind him, its handle quivering. Mr. Green turned and ran.

But as soon as he turned the corner, he stopped short. He listened. No one was coming.

Then he tiptoed into the Conservatory and ever so gently lifted the receiver from the telephone.

". . . Bring them to the mansion," he heard Miss Scarlet saying. She was speaking very quietly. Mr. Green had to press the receiver hard against his ear.

At that same moment, Mrs. White was in the Hall, dusting the phone and humming to herself. She glanced around to make sure no one was watching. Then she stopped dusting the phone, picked up the receiver, and heard Miss Scarlet say —

"Tonight at one. I'll leave the front door open. You can hide the rubies in the cookie jar in the Kitchen. Oh, don't worry. No one will look in there. All of Boddy's guests are on diets."

The two people who were eavesdropping on the extensions made horrible faces. They were about to shout at Miss Scarlet. But they remembered to keep quiet.

At the same moment, Mrs. Peacock entered the Study and crossed quickly to the phone. She was about to pick it up when Professor Plum entered.

"Ah," he said, "you're about to use the phone."

"Not at all," Mrs. Peacock said. "I was just looking at it. It's so . . . tasteful."

Professor Plum studied the phone. "Yes, I see what you mean," he said, totally bewildered.

"Did *you* want to make a call?" Mrs. Peacock asked.

"Ah! Thanks for reminding me!" Plum picked up the extension. Scowling and muttering at Plum's ill manners, Mrs. Peacock stomped out of the room.

"Are you clear on the plan?" Plum heard Miss Scarlet say. "Good, very very good. Soon those precious jewels will be mine!"

Just then, Mustard — who was left alone in the Library — picked up the Library extension. "Don't worry," he heard Miss Scarlet say. "No one's eavesdropping. I'm sure of it. All the guests are busy. That crazy Colonel is fighting one of his duels again."

Mustard stared at the phone in horror. He was about to challenge the phone to a duel, but he forced himself to stay silent.

Just then, Mrs. Peacock picked up the extension in the Billiard Room. She was so excited, the peacock feather on her head was twitching like crazy.

"Good-bye," she heard Miss Scarlet say.

And then she heard five clicks.

That night at one . . .

That night at one, a horrible rainstorm lashed the mansion. Lightning cracked, thunder boomed. When Boddy's grandfather's clock bonged once in the Lounge, the sound was drowned out by a thunderclap.

But as the clock struck one, the front door of Boddy's mansion swung open. A figure dressed in black hurried inside. He was dripping wet. And he was carrying a small paper bag. He shined his flashlight around the dark Hall, trying to find his way.

Just then, his soggy paper bag ripped open. Gleaming red rubies spilled out across the floor.

Cursing under his breath, the man quickly gathered the red rubies. Then he tiptoed to the Kitchen and hid the rubies in the cookie jar as instructed. Then he tiptoed back out the front door.

* * *

But . . .

But, just as the man was leaving, a guest began creeping down the front stairs. This guest headed straight for the Kitchen. The guest's hand was in the cookie jar when the Kitchen lights flicked on.

"Aha!" cried the guest who stood in the Kitchen doorway. "Trying to steal Scarlet's rubies, eh? I caught you, you thief!"

"You caught yourself," the first thief told him. "You overhead Miss Scarlet's phone call just like I did. You're down here for the same reason I am. C'mon, let's split the loot!"

NAME THE TWO THIEVES.

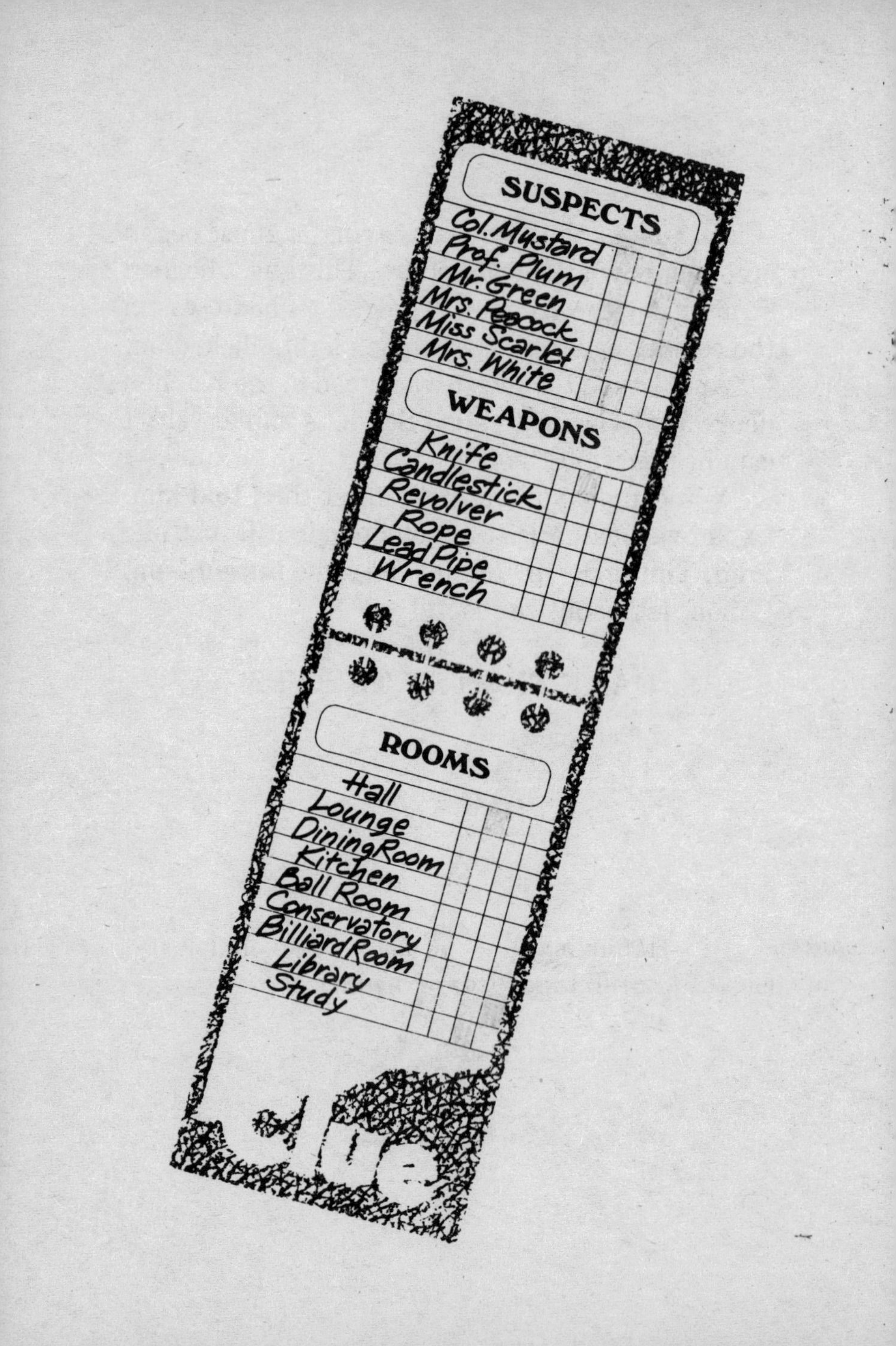
SUSPECTS
Col. Mustard
Prof. Plum
Mr. Green
Mrs. Peacock
Miss Scarlet
Mrs. White
WEAPONS
Knife
Candlestick
Revolver
Rope
Lead Pipe
Wrench
ROOMS
Hall
Lounge
Dining Room
Kitchen
Ball Room
Conservatory
Billiard Room
Library
Study
clue

SOLUTION

MRS. WHITE and MR. GREEN in the KITCHEN

They are the only two guests to pick up the phone early enough to hear Scarlet's hiding place. Unfortunately, the joke was on them.

Miss Scarlet wasn't talking about real rubies, she was talking about her favorite brand of jelly beans. The man on the phone was the candy store's delivery man. The only reason Miss Scarlet was being so secretive was to make sure no one else ate any of her precious sweets.

Mrs. White and Mr. Green got away with their crime, but they ruined their diets.

3
Wear Are the Weapons?

"AND NOW," CALLED MR. BODDY, "AS A special treat for my darling guests . . ."

Carrying a tray of pastries, and beaming from ear to ear, Mr. Boddy opened the Ball Room door. Just as —

The Revolver fired.

The bullet zoomed straight at Boddy's chest and —

ZING!

It struck the metal tray.

The pastries went flying, sticking all over Boddy's face and clothes. But at least the bullet had been stopped. Boddy was unharmed.

"Blast!" cursed Mustard. "Mr. Boddy, look what you've done! You got in the way. And I would have had a bull's-eye, too!"

Shaking, Mr. Boddy moved from the door. In the center of the door, Colonel Mustard had hung a small target. All the guests were lined up beside the Colonel, ready to take their turns.

"You know," Boddy said, wiping cream puff

icing from his nose, "I don't think target shooting inside the mansion is really such a good idea, and — "

Mr. Boddy was interrupted by the sound of Miss Scarlet, clapping her hands and laughing with glee. She was inspecting the target. "I win! I win!" she chanted.

Mustard turned yellow. "You can't be serious, Miss Scarlet. My last shot is obviously a do-over. Interference by Boddy."

Miss Scarlet crossed her arms. "Rules are rules. Game's over. I win."

"That's CHEATING!" Mustard shouted. "I challenge you to a duel!"

"Now, now," Mr. Boddy said, "there's no need to — "

"Nyah, nyah, Mustard lost," teased Green.

"Teasing?" said Mustard. "I challenge you to a duel, too!"

"A dual duel, eh?" asked Mrs. Peacock, laughing at her own joke.

"Laughing at me?" bellowed Mustard. "I challenge you to a triple duel!"

"Please!" yelled Mr. Boddy, dropping to his knees. "No more fighting!"

But within seconds, all the guests were fighting like crazy. Weapons flew through the air.

"STOP!" shouted Boddy.

The guests weren't used to hearing their mild-mannered host raise his voice. They all stopped fighting at once.

"Uh, Mr. Boddy," began Colonel Mustard. "We're all rather busy fighting right now, so if it's not important — "

"IT *IS* IMPORTANT!" Boddy ranted. "EVERYONE DROP YOUR WEAPONS!"

The guests weren't used to hearing their mild-mannered host raise his voice twice in a row. They all did as they were told.

Mr. Boddy was trembling, but he tried to keep his voice under control. "I simply will not tolerate any more fighting," he said. "And I have a solution to the problem." He flung open the Ball Room window.

"Oh, Reginald," Miss Scarlet called, swooning. "Don't jump."

"I'm not going to throw myself out the window!" Boddy said. "I want you to *throw your weapons* out the window. As of right this second, I am banning weapons from the mansion."

The guests looked stunned.

"Um, it's a good idea," Professor Plum began, "but . . . but what was the idea again?"

"It won't work," Green scoffed. "How will you enforce it?"

"I've thought of that," Mr. Boddy said. "I want you all to promise, scout's honor. Do you promise to be good and obey the rules?"

"We promise," said the guests, holding their crossed fingers behind their backs.

One after another, the guests threw their weapons out the window. Boddy closed the window and locked it.

"Good," he said. "That solves that problem." He breathed a deep sigh of relief, confident that his guests would never fight again.

That night . . .

That night, Mr. Boddy walked from room to room of his mansion. *Peace at last*, he thought. It was a wonderful thing. Without their weapons, his guests appeared to be getting along much, much better.

In the Conservatory, he found Colonel Mustard chatting with Miss Scarlet. Both were laughing gaily.

"You see," said Boddy, putting an arm around each of his guests, "isn't life better now without those awful weapons?"

The two guests agreed that it was.

"Oh my, what a beautiful and unusual necklace you're wearing," Boddy told Miss Scarlet.

"Oh, I'm glad you like it," Miss Scarlet cooed. "I wore it just for you."

"Yes . . . well . . . it's . . ." He let the sentence drift off. He actually thought the necklace was hideous. It was brown and was wrapped around her neck again and again. It looked like a Rope! But he certainly wasn't going to insult Miss Scarlet's taste in jewelry, not when the guests were all getting along so well.

"And you've got yourself a new eyepiece," Boddy told Mustard.

"What?" Mustard asked. "Oh, this? No, it's the same old monocle. But the string fell off. So I attached a new handle."

Mustard's monocle was clamped between the metal teeth of a long, silver handle. For one second, Mr. Boddy thought the handle looked familiar. It looked almost like a Wrench. But he shook the thought from his mind. "Very handsome," Boddy said.

"Glad you like it, old boy," said Mustard.

In the Ball Room, Boddy found Mrs. White doing some vacuuming, for once. "Mrs. White!" gasped Boddy. "What's gotten into you? You're working!"

"Yes. Just cleaning up those pastries from this afternoon," she explained with a polite smile. "You probably don't know this about me. But I just love doing chores." Then she turned her back and made a face as if she were throwing up.

Mr. Boddy was studying the vacuum cleaner.

"This looks new," he said, pointing to a long section of Lead Pipe.

"Uh, yes," said Mrs. White. "I added a new attachment. It's designed especially for sucking cream puffs out of the carpet."

"Ah," Boddy said, pleased. "Well, carry on."

Boddy was feeling even happier when he went into the Lounge. Plum and Mrs. Peacock were snacking on popcorn and laughing happily as they watched a horror movie on TV. "Mr. Plum," said Boddy, "you've changed your purple bow tie for once."

"Yes, yes," Plum said. "I thought it was time for a change."

In place of the purple bow tie, Plum was wearing a long, straight silver tie. The tie looked so shiny it was almost like metal. "It sure comes to a sharp point," Mr. Boddy said, gingerly touching the tie's tip.

"Yes, well," Plum said. "I tied the tie in a double-Windsor-sharp-point knot."

"I must learn that knot someday," said Boddy. "And Mrs. Peacock . . . look at *you*. You've put on a new hat."

"No, no," Mrs. Peacock said, blushing blue. "Just a new feather."

"Ah, quite right," agreed Boddy. Instead of the peacock feather, Mrs. Peacock's new feather was tall and straight and made of brass.

In the Billiard Room, Boddy found Green shooting pool. There was a special handle on the end of Green's cue stick.

"The trigger helps my aim enormously," Mr. Green explained, missing his shot. "Now look what you did!" He started toward his host.

"Sorry, Mr. Green, I didn't mean to, I — "

"Bother me again," Mr. Green warned, "and I'll twist your nose."

"Sorry," Boddy said. He quickly left the room.

But even Mr. Green couldn't ruin Boddy's mood. The guests were all happy and at peace; that was all that mattered. Feeling happy and at peace himself, Mr. Boddy wandered into the Study for a relaxing little snooze.

Which is when he heard noises coming from the Dining Room.

First there was a gunshot.

Followed by a piercing scream.

Then there was a thud and a groan.

He heard a man shout, "I've been clonked! That was hard!"

Later, when he tried to sort out what had happened, he found that one of the guests who had been in the Conservatory had used the secret passageway to cross to the Lounge.

And then one of the two women in the Lounge

had gone into the Dining Room.

At the same time, the guest with the Revolver had also entered the Dining Room. But what had happened next?

WHO SHOT WHOM?
AND WHO GOT CLONKED?

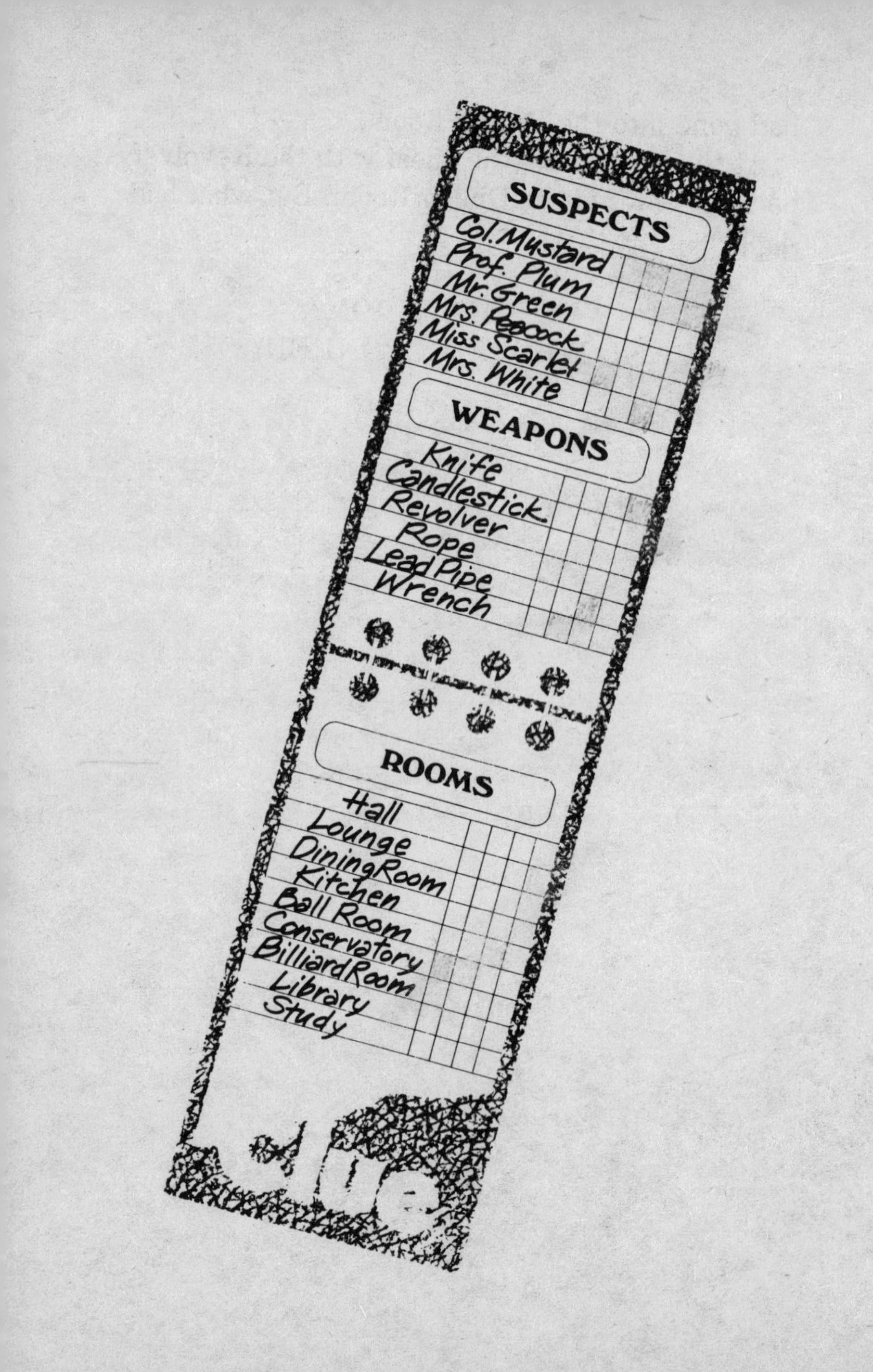
SUSPECTS
Col. Mustard
Prof. Plum
Mr. Green
Mrs. Peacock
Miss Scarlet
Mrs. White
WEAPONS
Knife
Candlestick
Revolver
Rope
Lead Pipe
Wrench
ROOMS
Hall
Lounge
Dining Room
Kitchen
Ball Room
Conservatory
Billiard Room
Library
Study
Clue

SOLUTION

MR. GREEN in the DINING ROOM shot MRS. PEACOCK with the REVOLVER. PEACOCK clonked GREEN with the CANDLESTICK.

The only weapon with a trigger is the Revolver. So we know that it was Mr. Green who did the shooting.

Since two women ended up in the Lounge, we know it was Miss Scarlet who left the Conservatory, not Mustard. And by the process of elimination, we know that Peacock is wearing the Candlestick instead of her usual peacock feather. So the weapons in the Lounge are the Rope, the Knife, and the Candlestick. Of those three weapons, only the Candlestick could be used for clonking.

Luckily for Mrs. Peacock, Green missed with his Revolver shot. Unluckily for Green, Mrs. Peacock didn't miss with her Candlestick.

Mr. Green was so dazed that for one hour he forgot to be a bully and was nice to everyone.

4
Blackout!

THE DOORBELL AT BODDY'S MANSION rang long and hard. Mrs. White opened the door to let in Mr. Green. He was wearing a green tuxedo and carrying a small green bag.

She curtsied low. "Welcome to Mr. Boddy's party," she said graciously. She had bowed so low that her face — and her sneer — were hidden from view.

Behind her, the other guests gathered in the Hall to greet the new arrival.

"Evening everybody," Green said. "I'm the last one to arrive, huh? Well, it's good to save the best for last." He chuckled in an unpleasant manner, his eyes and wrists sparkling.

Then he stopped laughing — right in the middle of a chuckle. "Staring at my wrists, eh?" he asked quietly. He held up his wrists so everyone could get a better look. "Go ahead and stare," he said.

The guests stared.

"Yup," he said. "They're solid gold cufflinks, worth ten grand apiece. Bought 'em just today."

The other guests whistled. "What's the occasion?" Miss Scarlet asked, her eyes still fixed on Green's sparkling jewelry.

"The occasion?" Plum asked. "Mr. Boddy's party?"

Ignoring the professor, Green explained to Miss Scarlet, "I made a *killing* on a business deal today."

"I'll bet you did," Mrs. Peacock observed. "A *real* killing."

"Jealous, aren't you?" asked Green in an oily voice. "Well, you should be." He laughed until he wheezed.

Mrs. White was reaching slowly toward Green's right wrist. He jerked his wrist away. "What do you think you're doing?" he growled.

"Um, you have a spot of lint on your sleeve," Mrs. White explained, picking up an imaginary piece of lint. "See?"

"I see all right," Green said. "And I'm warning all of you right now — "

Mr. Boddy clapped his hands together. "Well," he said, clearing his throat loudly. "This calls for a celebration! Mrs. White? I'd like to have a champagne toast for Mr. Green in the Dining Room."

"Very good, sir," she said, ever so politely.

"And put this bag in the Lounge for me, would

you, Mrs. White?" ordered Mr. Green.

"Very good, sir," she said, ever so politely.

Mr. Boddy gave his maid a surprised look. She sounded so polite, she almost didn't sound like herself.

And then she said, "Very good, sir," ever so politely again . . . and again. But her lips weren't moving.

Mrs. White quickly reached down to click off the mini-tape recorder she had hidden in her sleeve. "Whoops," she said, giving everyone an embarrassed smile.

Ten minutes later . . .

Ten minutes later, all the guests gathered in the Dining Room. Mrs. White wheeled in a cart with champagne in a bucket and seven crystal glasses.

"Ah," Boddy said. "Thank you, Mrs. White."

"You're welcome," the maid said as she aimed the champagne bottle right at Mr. Green.

Bang! She popped the cork. It flew straight at Green's head.

He ducked. On the wall behind him was a painting of Mr. Boddy's father, Daddy Boddy. The cork hit Daddy Boddy in the nose, and stuck there.

"Sorry about that," Mrs. White said sweetly. "It just slipped out."

"Well, no harm done," Mr. Boddy said, trying not to look at the painting of his father. He lifted his glass of champagne. "Well," he said. "I'm no good at public speaking — "

"You can say that again," said Mr. Green happily.

Mr. Boddy blushed. "Yes, well, anyway . . . I'm sure I speak for all of us, Mr. Green, when I say that I'm just so happy for you."

The other guests smiled at Mr. Green, keeping their hands — and their weapons — behind their backs.

"Cheers!" Mr. Boddy said, raising his glass.

"Gee, thanks," said Mr. Green. He clapped Mr. Boddy on the back so hard, Mr. Boddy spilled his champagne.

And at that exact moment —

The lights went off all over the mansion.

The guests groaned.

"Don't be alarmed," Mr. Boddy said in the darkness. "We must have blown a fuse."

Then he screamed.

All the guests screamed, as well.

"Sorry," Boddy said. "I just remembered that I'm terrified of the dark. But I'm — I'm fine now."

"A blackout," purred Miss Scarlet in the darkness. "How romantic."

There was the sound of someone snoring. Colonel Mustard chuckled. "I think Plum's gone to sleep."

"Mrs. White?" Mr. Boddy said. "Would you get everyone a candle?"

"Of course, Mr. Boddy," said the maid agreeably. Just then, the lights flicked back on, revealing Mrs. White with a horrible sneer on her face.

Mr. Boddy screamed again.

That woke up Plum. "Good morning," he said brightly.

And then the lights flickered off again.

And Plum went back to snoring.

"Well," Boddy said. "If everyone will just stay where they are, I'll go check the fuse box."

"And I'll get the candles," promised Mrs. White.

Mr. Boddy groped his way out of the Dining Room. He moved slowly through the hallway, waving his hands in front of him until he found the door to the basement.

He twisted the doorknob hard.

Only then did he remember that doorknobs are hard, not soft. And doorknobs aren't at nose level. And they don't tickle.

Mrs. Peacock screamed. "What are you doing?" she asked. "Let go of my nose!"

Mr. Boddy let go. "Sorry," he whimpered. "But I — I can't see a thing, and I'm — I'm — "

"Scared?" Mrs. Peacock asked.

Mr. Boddy nodded.

"Well, answer me!" said Mrs. Peacock, who couldn't see him nodding in the dark. "How rude!"

"I'm scared," Mr. Boddy said.

Then he screamed again as someone took his hand.

"It's just me," Mrs. Peacock said with a sigh. "C'mon, I'll go with you to the basement."

Meanwhile, back in the Dining Room . . .

Meanwhile, back in the Dining Room, Mr. Green had become very worried and suspicious. *Maybe this blackout is no accident*, he thought. Then a light went on in his head, though the room remained pitch-dark. He had it. Maybe someone was after his cufflinks!

"Out of my way!" he yelled, shoving through the dark room.

"Hey!" Plum cried. "Careful! I'm napping!"

But Green didn't stop. He ran through the pitch-black mansion, heading for the Lounge. He needed his green bag. That is, he needed what was *inside* his green bag — his Revolver.

But on his way to the Lounge, Green ran into Mustard.

He ran into him so hard that Mustard was knocked unconscious.

Feeling his way along the wall, Green continued on his way to the Lounge.

He found his bag.

Reached into it.

Only to feel the hand of another guest closing around the Revolver's wooden handle.

"I just thought you might need the gun to protect yourself," Miss Scarlet purred in the darkness.

"Sure you did," Green sneered.

She handed him the Revolver. "I'll stay right by your side," she promised. "I've got the Wrench, so I can help protect you. I don't trust these other guests. Someone might try to take advantage of the blackout and steal your cufflinks."

"Oh, gee, I hadn't thought of that," Green said sarcastically.

"You don't have to be nasty," said Miss Scarlet. "I'm only trying to be helpful." She tried to run her fingers through his hair but, because of the darkness, she missed and poked him right in the eye.

"Ow!" yelled Green. "I can't see a thing!"

"That's because it's a blackout," Miss Scarlet

reminded him. "Please let me go with you and protect you."

"All right," growled Green. "Follow me. I'm going to try to get to my car."

Miss Scarlet linked her arm through his. Green started toward the door. He found the doorway and went through.

"Oof!"

Miss Scarlet, who was by his side, had walked straight into the wall.

"Sorry about that," Green said, helping her back to her feet.

"No harm done," Miss Scarlet said huskily.

They groped their way toward the Hall. But in the dark, they got confused and ended up outside the Kitchen instead.

Now it was Mr. Green and Miss Scarlet who screamed. Inside the Kitchen, they could see Mrs. White lighting the candle in the Candlestick. Lit from below, Mrs. White's face glowed like a menacing ghost.

Just then —

Someone came up behind Green and Scarlet and —

RIP! RIP! Mr. Green felt something rip his sleeves.

"Stop, thief!" Green shouted. He fired his Revolver uselessly into the darkness.

Then the lights came back on. The bullets had

plugged two more holes into the portrait of Daddy Boddy in the Dining Room. And there were two holes in Green's sleeves.

Green's cufflinks were gone.

NAME THE THIEF.

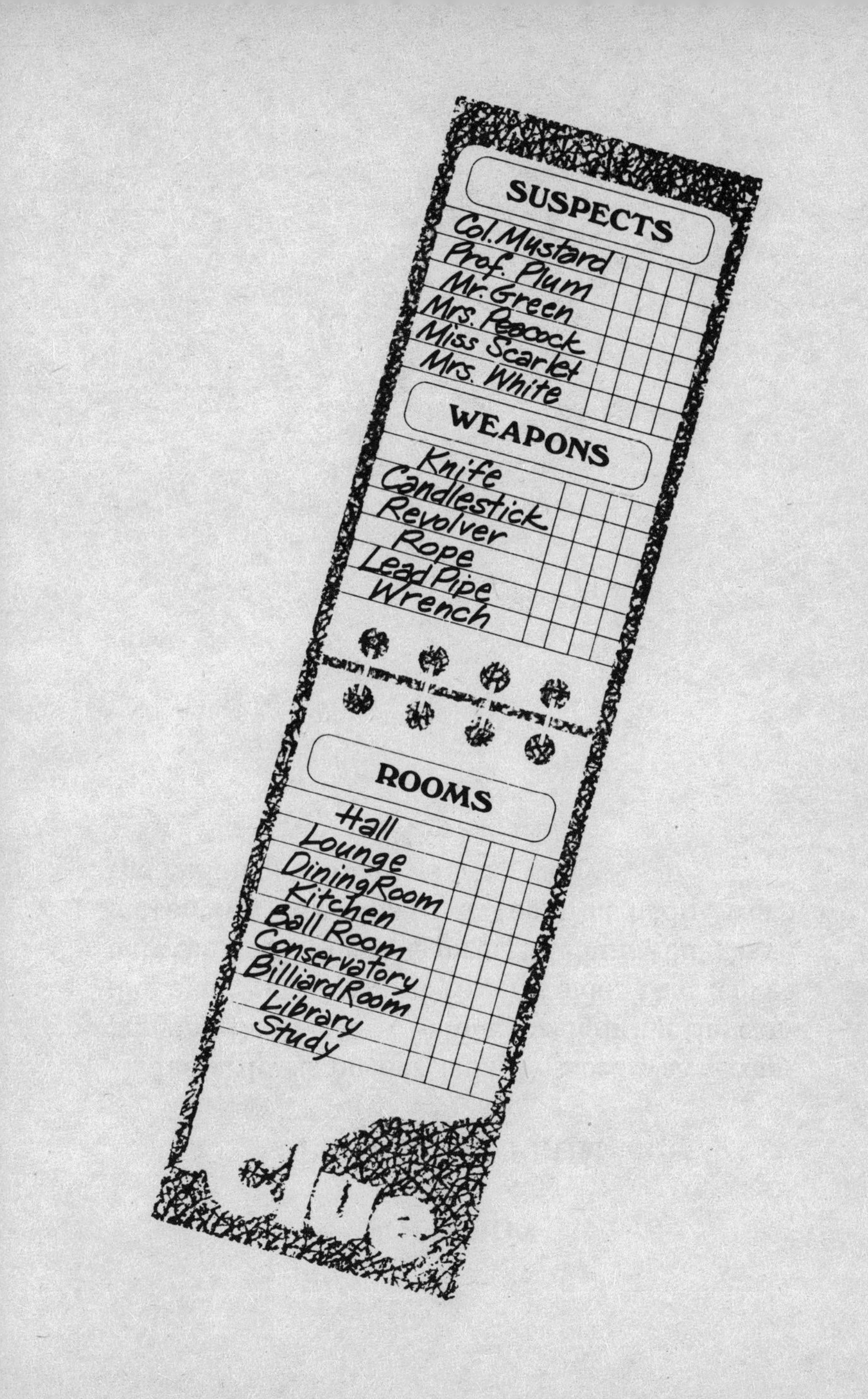
SUSPECTS
Col. Mustard
Prof. Plum
Mr. Green
Mrs. Peacock
Miss Scarlet
Mrs. White
WEAPONS
Knife
Candlestick
Revolver
Rope
Lead Pipe
Wrench
ROOMS
Hall
Lounge
Dining Room
Kitchen
Ball Room
Conservatory
Billiard Room
Library
Study

42

SOLUTION

PROFESSOR PLUM

Mustard was unconscious, Peacock was accompanying Boddy, Mrs. White was lighting the candle, and Scarlet was at Green's side. That leaves only the Professor. The forgetful Plum would have gotten away with his theft, too, if he hadn't worn the cufflinks to Boddy's next party.

5
The Walls Have Eyes

IT WAS A COLD AND RAINY NIGHT. The grandfather clock in Boddy's Ball Room chimed eight times. It was seven o'clock.

Just then, a figure dressed in black tiptoed into the room. A thief! The thief looked right, left, up, down.

Sure that no one was watching, the thief removed a painting from the wall. Behind the painting was a safe. "Looks safe," said the thief, glancing around again.

With a black-gloved hand, the thief now pulled out a silver Wrench. The silvery Wrench shined silver in the silvery streetlight that shone through the silver window above the window sill.

"Silver," murmured the thief, eyeing the safe. "The silver is mine!"

Then the thief tried to wrench open the safe.

On the wall to the thief's left hung a portrait

of Mr. Boddy's mother, Bessie Boddy. Oddly enough, whenever the thief moved, the eyes of the painting moved as well — watching.

The eyes belonged to Mrs. Peacock. She was standing outside the Ball Room, staring through the secret peepholes in the painting — and spying on the thief.

Excellent, thought Mrs. Peacock as she watched the thief at work. *Now I can do a little blackmail!* She would demand half the thief's loot, in return for not revealing the thief's identity.

Unfortunately for Mrs. Peacock, she wasn't the only one who was spying. One of the guests was holding his monocle up to the secret peephole in the Conservatory wall. Colonel Mustard was spying on Mrs. Peacock.

"Excellent," whispered Mustard. "Just smashing." So Mrs. Peacock was spying on one of the guests, wasn't she? She was probably planning to do a little blackmail, wasn't she?

"Then I'll blackmail Mrs. Peacock," murmured Mustard. "Either she pays me a lot of money, or I tell everyone she was spying."

It was a perfect plan. There was just one little problem. Unfortunately for the Colonel, he was also being watched.

The door to the secret passageway to the

Lounge lay open. In the Lounge, one of the other guests had set up her telescope. The telescope was focused right on Mustard. *Excellent*, thought the guest. *Now I can blackmail the Colonel!*

But this guest was being watched as well.

By Mr. Green, who was hiding behind the two-way mirror on the Lounge dresser.

Excellent, thought Mr. Green, happily rubbing his hands together. *Now I can do a little blackmail!*

But just then —

A voice behind Mr. Green murmured, "See anything interesting?"

Mr. Green jumped. "Ah, Miss Scarlet," said Green, turning blue. "How nice of you to sneak up behind me and nearly give me a heart attack."

Miss Scarlet laughed. "And I suppose what *you're* doing is nice?"

"I don't know what you mean. I was just playing a little hide-and-seek," Green explained nervously.

Miss Scarlet glanced to the left and right. The hallway was deserted. "Are you playing by yourself?" she asked, arching an eyebrow.

"Yes . . . er . . . couldn't get anyone else to play," said Green.

"Well then," said Miss Scarlet as she struggled to get her eyebrow to stop arching. "It's a good thing I found you!"

WHO IS THE THIEF?

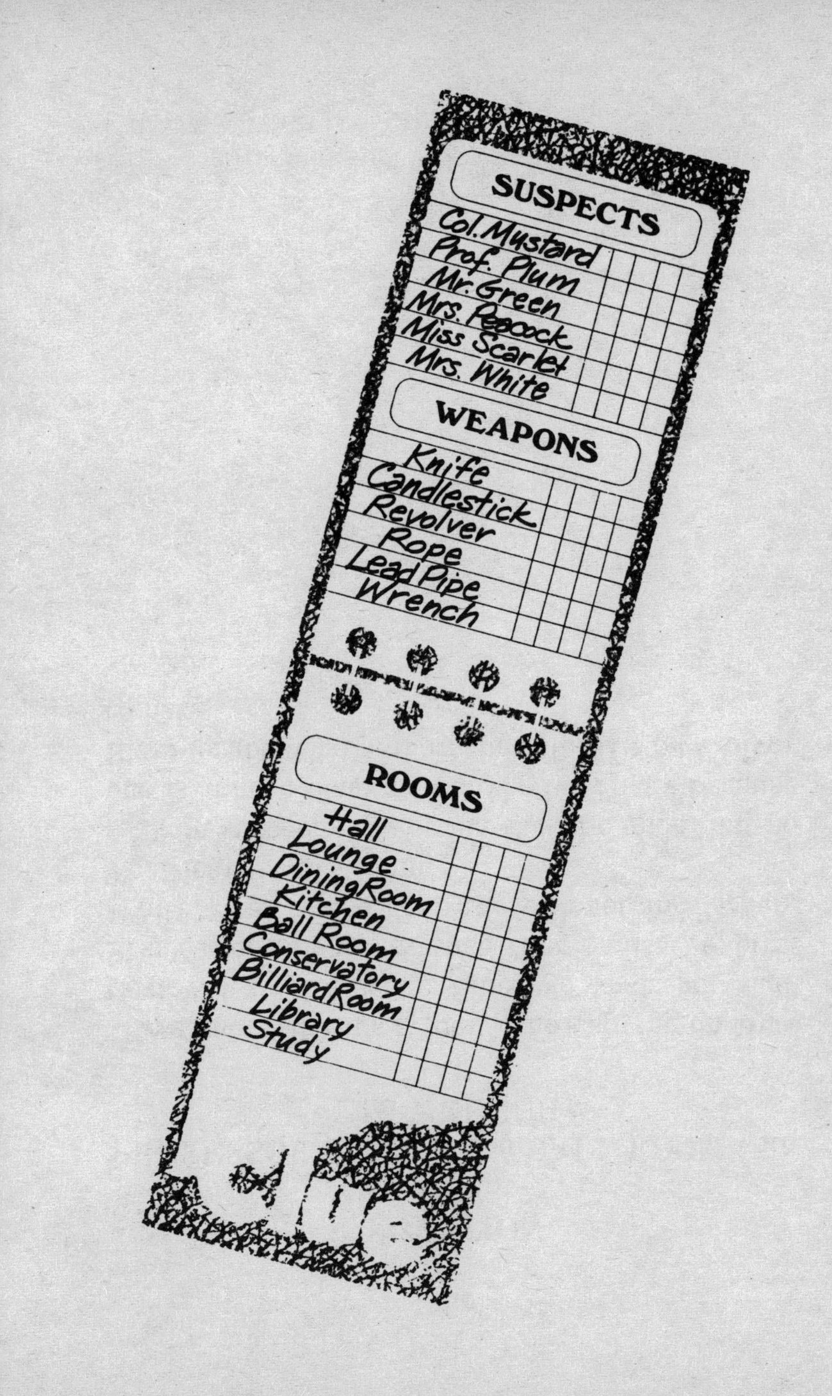
SUSPECTS
Col. Mustard
Prof. Plum
Mr. Green
Mrs. Peacock
Miss Scarlet
Mrs. White
WEAPONS
Knife
Candlestick
Revolver
Rope
Lead Pipe
Wrench
ROOMS
Hall
Lounge
Dining Room
Kitchen
Ball Room
Conservatory
Billiard Room
Library
Study
clue

48

SOLUTION

PROFESSOR PLUM in the BALL ROOM with the WRENCH

We know that it's a "her" who's spying on Mustard with the telescope. Since we've already seen Scarlet and Peacock, that "her" must be Mrs. White. We've also seen the Colonel and Green. That leaves only Plum.

Plum succeeds in getting the safe open, but no one is able to blackmail anybody. That's because Plum forgot what was *in* the safe. His *own* silver coins!

6
The Guest Who Stole Christmas

SNOW WAS FALLING. THE PRETTY LITtle flakes were dusting Boddy's mansion like sugar on a cookie.

Mr. Boddy had spent the day on a ladder, draping the mansion with Christmas lights: red, green, purple, yellow, white, and peacock-blue. His work had paid off. Now the vast building blinked merrily in the darkness.

On the doorstep of the mansion stood a large scarlet reindeer, ringing the doorbell.

Mr. Boddy flung open the door. He was dressed in a Santa suit, complete with fluffy white beard. "Merry Christmas and welcome to my party!" he cried happily. "And who are you dressed up as, Miss Scarlet?"

"Scarlet the scarlet-nosed reindeer," Miss Scarlet said with a wink. "Who else?"

"Ho, ho, ho!" chortled Boddy merrily. He hooked his arm through hers. "Follow me!" he cried.

He led her to the Study, where Mrs. White was serving eggnog to the other guests.

Miss Scarlet wasn't the only guest who had shown up in costume. Professor Plum was dressed as a purple skeleton. When he saw Miss Scarlet and Boddy, Plum raised his glass of eggnog. "Happy Halloween," he toasted proudly.

"Ho, ho, ho," laughed Boddy. "What a kidder."

"Wonderful party, old boy," Colonel Mustard called to Boddy. "And what a beautiful tree!"

Boddy beamed, his eyes as shiny as two Christmas tree ornaments. The tree stood in the corner, blinking, shining, gleaming, sparkling, glimmering, and twinkling. And underneath the tree lay large shiny presents for all the guests. The gifts were wrapped in blue, white, purple, green, scarlet, and mustard-yellow.

"I think I can guess which present is for me," Professor Plum said, eyeing the green present and drooling.

"What did you get us?" Mrs. Peacock demanded. "It's not polite to keep secrets, you know."

"Now, now," Boddy said, pulling at his fake beard and grinning. "It's only Thursday. Christmas Eve is a day away. You'll just have to wait."

Mr. Green was standing near the crackling fire. Nailed to the fireplace were six bulging stockings: blue, white, purple, green, scarlet, and yellow. "And what have we here?" he called eagerly, dollar signs flashing in his eyes.

"Now, now — no peeking," Mr. Boddy said, leading Mr. Green away from the stockings.

"Oh, I'm so excited," Mrs. White exclaimed as she drained her glass of eggnog. Hidden behind the glass, she rolled her eyes.

"I'll bet you are," said Boddy. "Tell me, Mrs. White. What do you want for Christmas?"

Mrs. White smiled brightly. "Just working for you is enough of a present, Mr. Boddy," she said as she pickpocketed Boddy's wallet.

"Oh, Reginald," Miss Scarlet said, "you really shouldn't have gone to all this trouble." She pick-pocketed the wallet from Mrs. White as she said it. Turning aside, she glanced quickly into the wallet. Empty! She tossed the wallet into the fire, where it sizzled.

"Yes, yes," Boddy said. "I suppose you're right, Miss Scarlet. I really overdid it this year. Can you imagine? I haven't got a penny left in the house. I spent a million dollars!"

All the guests froze, their glasses of eggnog poised in midair.

"But," said Boddy, "I just couldn't help it. The thought of having all my favorite friends here for Christmas . . . it was just so special!"

"Very special," agreed Mustard, loading his weapon behind his back.

"You're a true Santa Claus," added Miss Scarlet as she slipped the Knife into her scarlet purse.

Merry Mr. Boddy was too happy to notice. "Now," he said, "I know you're all dying to know what I got you. So, just to make sure there's no hanky-panky with the presents tonight while I'm asleep . . ."

He hoisted a large, red sack that had been sitting in the corner. Whatever was inside the sack clinked loudly. Boddy opened the sack and pulled out a giant padlock. ". . . I purchased these extra-heavy-duty locks," he explained.

"Oh, Mr. Boddy," the guests all said at once, "you don't have to do that. You can trust us!"

"I know, I know," said Boddy. "But just to be safe . . ." He began locking all the windows and the doors.

"But those padlocks have no keyholes," Mrs. White said.

"And no combination dials," added Mr. Green.

"Quite right," Boddy said. "They're a new kind of lock. They work on a timer system. They're set to open at midnight on Christmas Eve. And not a second before!"

The guests were all frowning.

"Now don't look so glum," Mr. Boddy said happily as he clicked the padlocks shut. "You'll enjoy your presents much more if you wait. By the way, you should know that these padlocks are absolutely unbreakable and foolproof."

"But Mr. Boddy," all the guests began at once.

But Mr. Boddy wouldn't listen. He ushered the guests from the room, and then —

Click.

He padlocked the door shut behind them.

But that night . . .

But that night, Mrs. Peacock tiptoed down the backstairs with the Wrench. She tightened the Wrench around the padlock on the Study door. She squeezed and twisted with all her might. She groaned. Boddy wasn't kidding. These locks were tough. How rude!

Mrs. Peacock was struggling so hard with the Study door, she didn't notice Professor Plum in his purple snowsuit, outside in the snow, tiptoeing past the window. Plum was carrying the Candlestick. With one sharp blow, he smashed the Library window. He let himself inside.

Then he remembered. The presents were in the Study.

Mrs. White didn't make the same mistake. She was outside the Study at that very moment, one of the weapons raised over her head. She smashed the weapon down against the glass of the Study window.

But the glass didn't break.

Then she saw the label stuck to the window. Mr. Boddy had thought of everything. He'd even installed shatterproof glass!

But at that same moment, one of the other guests had found a way to sneak into the Study. The guest was using the Rope to climb down the chimney like Santa Claus.

Some Santa. Instead of *bringing* presents, this Santa Claus stole every gift in every stocking and took all the boxes that were under the tree.

WHO STOLE THE GIFTS?

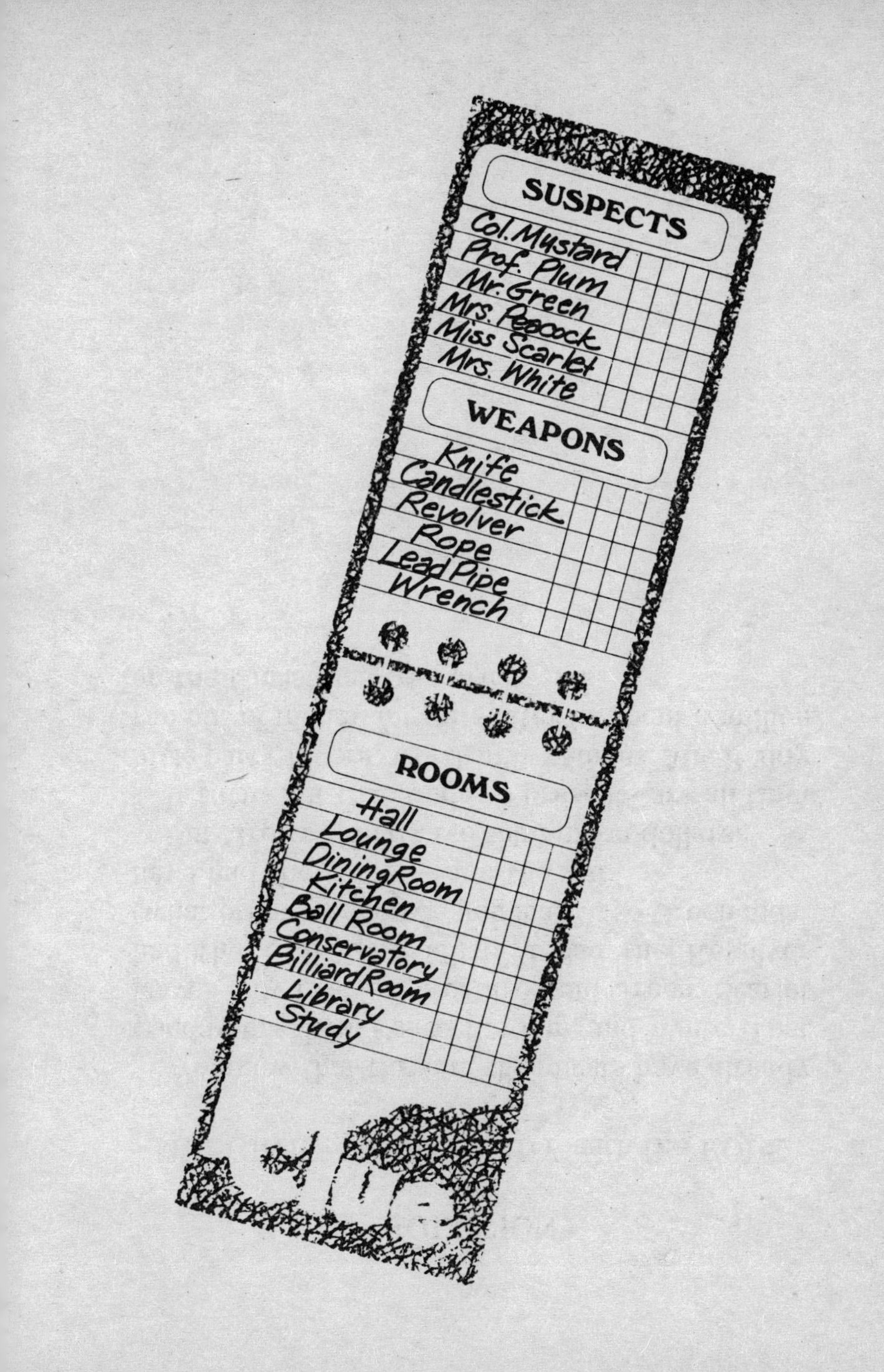

SUSPECTS
Col. Mustard
Prof. Plum
Mr. Green
Mrs. Peacock
Miss Scarlet
Mrs. White
WEAPONS
Knife
Candlestick
Revolver
Rope
Lead Pipe
Wrench
ROOMS
Hall
Lounge
DiningRoom
Kitchen
Ball Room
Conservatory
BilliardRoom
Library
Study

56

SOLUTION

MR. GREEN in the STUDY with the ROPE

We know that three of the guests have already tried to break in: Peacock, Plum, and White. That leaves only Scarlet, Mustard, and Green. Scarlet had the Knife and Mustard had the Revolver (what other weapon do you load?), so Green must have had the Rope — and the gifts.

But Green didn't have the million dollars.

It turns out that Boddy's presents are all tiny, little party favors, worth only pennies. Mr. Boddy ran out of money for gifts after he spent a million on the Christmas tree ornaments.

7
A Room With a View

IT WAS DUSK. MR. BODDY SIPPED HIS evening cup of tea as he gazed peacefully out the Dining Room window.

Such a beautiful view. The mansion's rolling green lawns . . . Mr. Boddy's priceless new rose beds . . . so gorgeous. Ahhhh, life, sighed Boddy.

Then he heard a horrible *putt-putt-putting*.

A plum-colored Volkswagen came into view.

Oh, no! thought Boddy. The car was headed right for the rose bed.

Mr. Boddy yelled a warning, but with the window shut there was no way he could be heard. The car drove right through the rose bed. Then it parked. The door opened. Out came Professor Plum.

"Ahhhhh, company," sighed Boddy, trying to stay calm. After all, only half his roses were ruined.

Then Plum opened the Volkswagen's other door. Out bounded a gigantic Great Dane with a purple collar. Plum grabbed for the dog . . . and missed. The Great Dane raced around the rose bed, tearing up the other half of the roses.

Meanwhile, in the Kitchen . . .

Meanwhile, in the Kitchen, Mrs. White was scraping those hard-to-get spots in her pots with the Knife. She paused to wipe her forehead. And as she did, she happened to glance out the window.

Her jaw dropped.

In the dusky darkness, she could just make out Miss Scarlet, tied to a tree with the Rope. Miss Scarlet appeared to be gagged with her own scarlet kerchief. She was kicking her legs frantically, but it was no use. She was tied fast.

Mrs. White smiled. "Serves you right," she said gleefully. She bent her head back to her work, pretending she hadn't seen a thing.

At the same time . . .

At the same time, in the Ball Room, Mrs. Peacock was playing her favorite Chopin *étude*. The peacock feather in her hat swished back and forth, back and forth, keeping the rhythm.

Suddenly, she stopped playing and made a face. The A-sharp was sounding more like A-flat. And the whole piano was sounding like A-piece of junk! Muttering, she took out the Wrench and started tuning the piano's strings. But as she leaned over the piano, something outside the Ball Room's bay windows caught her eye.

Her peacock feather stood up straight. Was her mind playing tricks on her? That would be very rude of her mind! She looked again. It was true!

Outside the window, in the dusky half light, there was a masked figure, digging in the dirt with the Lead Pipe.

Mrs. Peacock leaned forward for a better view. Now she saw that the figure was burying something . . .

She leaned further forward. . . .

It looked like . . .

She leaned further forward —

And fell face first on the floor in a lump. "That thief is burying a diamond necklace!" cried Mrs. Peacock into the carpet.

Meanwhile . . .

Meanwhile, Mrs. White was watching out the Kitchen window as Professor Plum untied Miss Scarlet. Scarlet pointed to her bare neck and then pointed to her left. Thinking quickly, Plum ran to his right.

Mrs. Peacock, meanwhile, was still watching through the Ball Room window. As she watched, the masked figure appeared to hear something from over by the Kitchen. He looked to his right, then ran off to his left.

Through the Dining Room window, Boddy saw Plum run into view. The Professor stopped, scratched his head, and ran the other way.

Meanwhile, in the Conservatory, a guest was balancing the Candlestick on his nose. It dropped. And when the guest bent to pick it up, he saw something outside the window that made him freeze.

A masked figure was running by. And as he ran, the masked figure pulled off the mask and tossed it into the bushes.

The eyesight of the guest in the Conservatory wasn't everything it should have been.

And it was getting darker and darker outside.

And the figure was running fast.

The guest in the Conservatory squinted. "Is that Mrs. Peacock?" he wondered aloud. "Boddy? Plum? Green? Mrs. White?"

WHO STOLE MISS SCARLET'S DIAMOND NECKLACE?

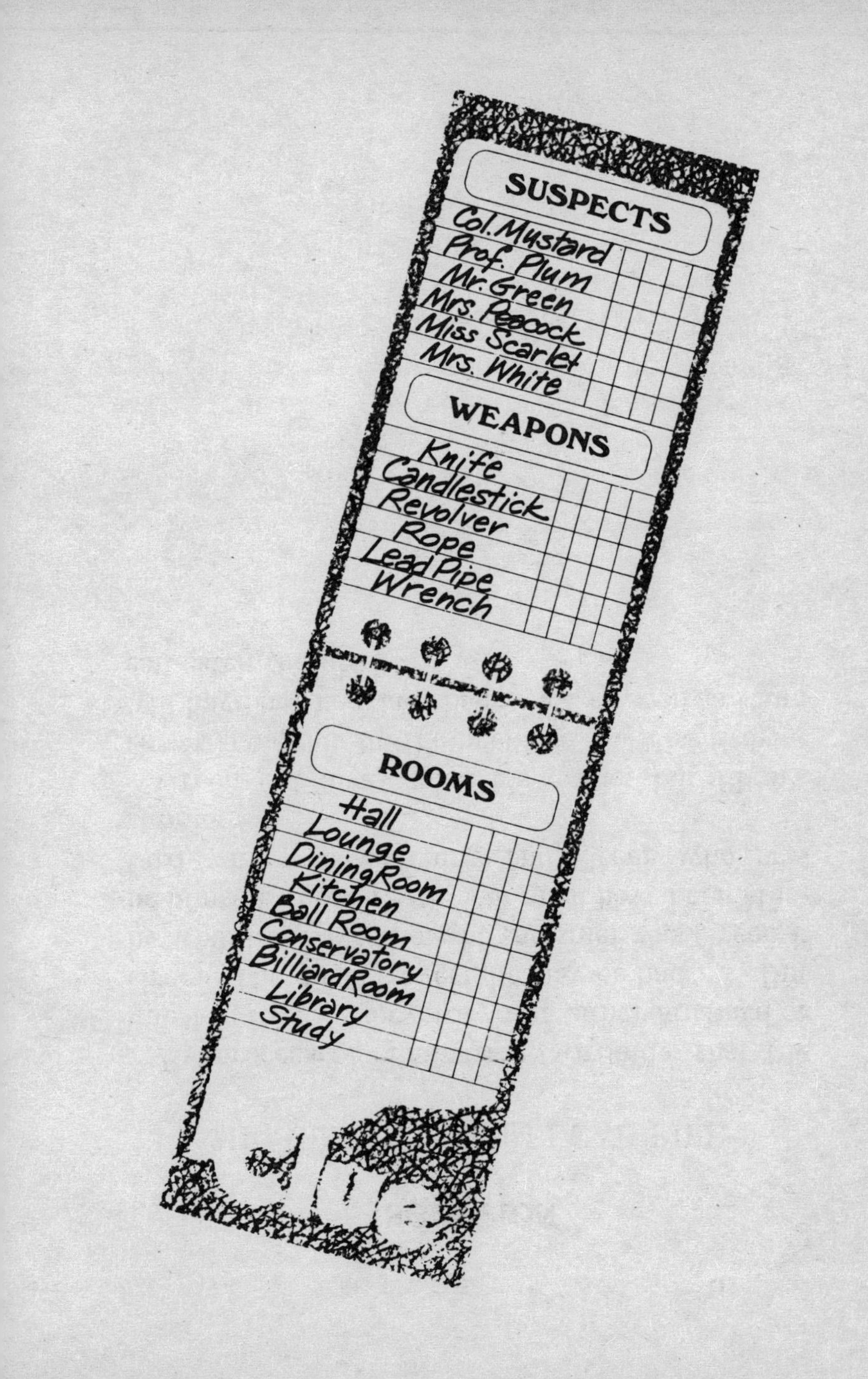

SUSPECTS
Col. Mustard
Prof. Plum
Mr. Green
Mrs. Peacock
Miss Scarlet
Mrs. White
WEAPONS
Knife
Candlestick
Revolver
Rope
Lead Pipe
Wrench
ROOMS
Hall
Lounge
Dining Room
Kitchen
Ball Room
Conservatory
Billiard Room
Library
Study

SOLUTION

MR. GREEN with the LEAD PIPE

By process of elimination, we know that the guest in the Conservatory was either Mustard or Green. The guest's eyesight may be bad . . . But he wouldn't have thought the thief was Green if he himself were Green. So it must have been Mustard who was watching and Green who was running.

Green got away with his crime, but Plum's Great Dane dug up the necklace. So Miss Scarlet will have her necklace back, just as soon as Plum can catch the dog!

8
The Guest Who Couldn't Shoot Straight

"I FEEL LIKE I'M FORGETTING SOMEthing," Professor Plum said.

"So what else is new?" quipped Miss Scarlet.

The two guests were sunning themselves on the plastic chaise longue chairs that Mr. Boddy had set up next to his swimmng pool. Miss Scarlet was wearing a scarlet bikini. Luckily for Plum, she was also wearing dark sunglasses. Because Plum was wearing nothing at all.

"What do you think of my new purple bathing suit?" Plum asked Scarlet.

"Lovely," Scarlet said, without bothering to look.

Just then, Professor Plum felt a slight chill. His face turned purple with embarrassment. "Excuse me just a moment," he said. He ran into the mansion, put on his purple suit, and returned to the pool.

"Isn't this relaxing?" asked Miss Scarlet, who didn't even notice that he'd been gone.

"Sure is," agreed Plum. He nervously slathered himself with purple sunscreen. "But I still have this nagging feeling that I'm forgetting something."

There was a loud snort from the woods surrounding the pool.

"Miss Scarlet!" exclaimed Plum. "There's no reason to snort at me, just because I have a poor memory!"

Miss Scarlet laughed. "I didn't snort, Professor. You did."

There was another snort, even louder than before. Miss Scarlet giggled. "Why, Professor, you sound just like that comedian on the radio. What's his name?" She snapped her fingers several times. "I'm getting as bad as you, Professor. His name escapes me."

Plum sat up straight. "Radio?" he asked. "Escape?"

"Huh?" said Miss Scarlet.

There was another snort from the woods.

"I almost had it there for a second," Plum said. "I think it was something on the radio. Some kind of emergency broadcast."

"Well at least it wasn't important," Miss Scarlet joked.

"I'd better go listen," Plum said, heading back into the mansion.

Miss Scarlet smiled. Alone at last. Total peace.

Snort!!

This was the loudest snort yet.

And the strange thing was . . .

Professor Plum had already gone inside. So who could . . .?

Miss Scarlet whipped off her sunglasses.

She couldn't believe her eyes. Did she have sun stroke? No, it was true. . . .

There was a wild rhinoceros charging out of the woods. And the huge, gray, horned beast was thundering straight toward her!

Screaming, Miss Scarlet ran off, pursued by a rhino.

For a moment, there was no one at the pool. The waves gently lapped the sides, and the sound of Miss Scarlet's screams faded into the summer air.

Then the mansion door opened and Professor Plum returned. "Miss Scarlet," he said, chuckling. "I've finally remembered what it was. I'm such a ninny. I forgot to mention that a wild rhino has escaped from the local zoo. It seems to be headed right this way, so we're all supposed to stay inside the mansion until further — " He stopped short and stared at the empty chaise longue.

"Humph. I must have already told her the message," he told himself. And with that, he headed back into the mansion.

Meanwhile, in the Library . . .

Meanwhile, in the Library, the other guests were all playing Crazy Eights. At least, that's what they were playing five minutes ago. Now they were all screaming and accusing each other of cheating. And one moment later, they began rolling around on the floor in one big tussle.

"Please," begged Mr. Boddy. "It's just a game of cards. It's not worth fighting over."

The guests paused to listen thoughtfully to their host. They all answered as one. "We disagree," said the guests. Then they whipped out their weapons and shouted at each other, "DIE, CHEATER!" and went back to fighting.

"Well!" said the poor host, crossing his arms. "You won't catch me fighting over a card game. No sir!"

Just then, the Library door flew open, knocking poor Boddy right into the tumble of fighting guests on the floor.

Professor Plum entered. "I have an important announcement to make," he announced. "And you all had better stop fighting and listen to me before I forget!"

But the guests didn't stop fighting. And sure enough, Plum forgot his announcement. He was so furious that he dived into the fray and joined the battle.

Just then, Miss Scarlet dove through the open window. "I'M BEING CHASED BY A WILD RHINO!" she screamed.

Everyone stopped fighting. And laughed.

"Miss Scarlet has lost her marbles," said Mrs. Peacock, giggling.

"A wild rhino! That is so nutty," forgetful Professor Plum agreed, laughing louder than anyone else.

He stopped laughing when the rhino crashed headfirst through the Library wall. But then the rhino got stuck. His head was inside the Library and the rest of his body was outside.

"That's odd," Plum said, stroking the rhino's horn. "I don't remember Mr. Boddy hanging a rhino's head in the Library."

"I didn't," Boddy said, trembling all over.

"Ah," said Plum. He thought quickly. "In that case . . . Colonel Mustard, is this one of *your* hunting trophies?"

Just then, the rhino snorted and tried to bite Plum's nose. Plum staggered back in fear. The frustrated rhino pulled his head out of the wall and disappeared.

"Oh, dear!" cried Boddy. "Everyone stay inside!" He ran to call the police.

"And you called me crazy," Miss Scarlet cried. "I'll kill you for that insult!" She charged at the other guests, who all resumed fighting.

Suddenly — *BANG!* — a Revolver was fired.

Once again, everyone stopped fighting. Colonel Mustard had his Revolver pointed straight up in the air. "My friends," he said. "I haven't hunted wild rhino since I was on safari in faraway Bagel-Bagel. We must organize a hunting party!"

Dashing Colonel Mustard dashed to his room. He returned a moment later, wearing a yellow pith helmet. He was carrying a large wooden box. Inside the box were six Revolvers. The handles were all different colors. There was a blue one, a green one, a scarlet one, a purple one, a white one, and a yellow one.

"I must warn you," said Mustard. "Not all of these pistols shoot straight. Two shoot to the left, two shoot to the right. Don't worry, the other two shoot perfectly."

"That's comforting," said Miss Scarlet.

Mustard handed Scarlet the yellow Revolver, warning her that it shot to the left.

He gave the green Revolver to Mrs. Peacock, warning her that it shot to the right.

He gave the blue Revolver to Mr. Green, telling him that it shot perfectly.

He gave the white Revolver to Plum, warning him that it shot to the left.

Then he gave one of the remaining two Revolvers to Mrs. White, telling her it also shot perfectly.

And then he led the guests out of the mansion and into the woods.

"I hope there's no poison ivy out here," Plum said.

"You're worrying about catching a rash?" snarled Green. "Why don't you worry about getting gored by a wild rhino?"

Plum shivered violently. "Why did you have to remind me?"

"That's one good thing about having a bad memory," commented Mrs. White. "Plum doesn't remember that we're all about to die."

"Courage, my hunters," said Mustard. "Courage. Gather round." No one moved.

"Now," said Mustard. "It's a well-known fact that an angry rhino will race around a mansion in circles, from right to left." He studied his watch. "Which means the rhino should be passing here in exactly . . . one minute. So . . ."

He looked up from his watch. The guests were all pointing their Revolvers at each other. And they had all gone back to arguing about the Crazy Eights game.

"Please," said Mustard. "We have only fifty seconds left. Fan out into your special rhino-hunting positions!"

But the guests stood right where they were, and they kept arguing.

Back in the mansion, Mr. Boddy raced into the Library. "The police and the zookeepers are on their way," he explained breathlessly. "They say we should stay inside. This rhinoceros is very deadly and — "

Mr. Boddy stopped midsentence. The room was empty. "Oh, no!" Boddy ran to the wall and peered out through the hole the rhino had made. He saw all the guests standing in the woods, pointing their Revolvers at each other. And charging straight toward them, was —

"THE RHINO!" Boddy screamed out the hole.

But the guests didn't hear him. They didn't even look up.

"Ten seconds!" Mustard shouted at his troops. "Take your positions!"

The guests didn't listen to the Colonel. But they did listen to the ground. The whole ground was thundering and shaking.

"THE RHINO!" screamed the guests.

And at last, the guests took their positions.

Well, not exactly. What really happened was the guests all turned and started to run.

"FIVE!" Mustard cried, studying his watch. "FOUR . . . THREE . . ."

The thunderous thundering of hooves grew even more thunderous and thundering.

Everyone stopped running and froze.

"HOLD YOUR FIRE, MEN!" roared Mustard. "UNTIL YOU SEE THE TIP OF THE RHINO'S — "

Before Mustard could shout the word "HORN" he, himself, saw the horn.

The long sharp horn of the rhino was charging right at him, only inches from his backside.

"Uh-oh," said Mustard. And then he started to run.

At the same instant, back in the mansion, poor Mr. Boddy covered his eyes.

The guests, meanwhile, all began firing like crazy.

But the rhino charged on.

A moment later, the thunderous thundering of hooves grew faint. All was silent.

"Blast!" Colonel Mustard cried, climbing down from a tree. "I was sure I'd bagged him!"

"That's all right," Mrs. White said. "We can hang Mr. Green's head on the wall instead!"

Colonel Mustard looked down. Sure enough, there lay Mr. Green. Shot!

Who shot Mr. Green?

No one knew.

The confusion of the hunting scene was too great for the guests to sort out the mystery.

The culprit was the guest with the purple Revolver.

The guest with the purple Revolver aimed straight at the rhino. But the shot hit Mr. Green instead.

WHO SHOT MR. GREEN?

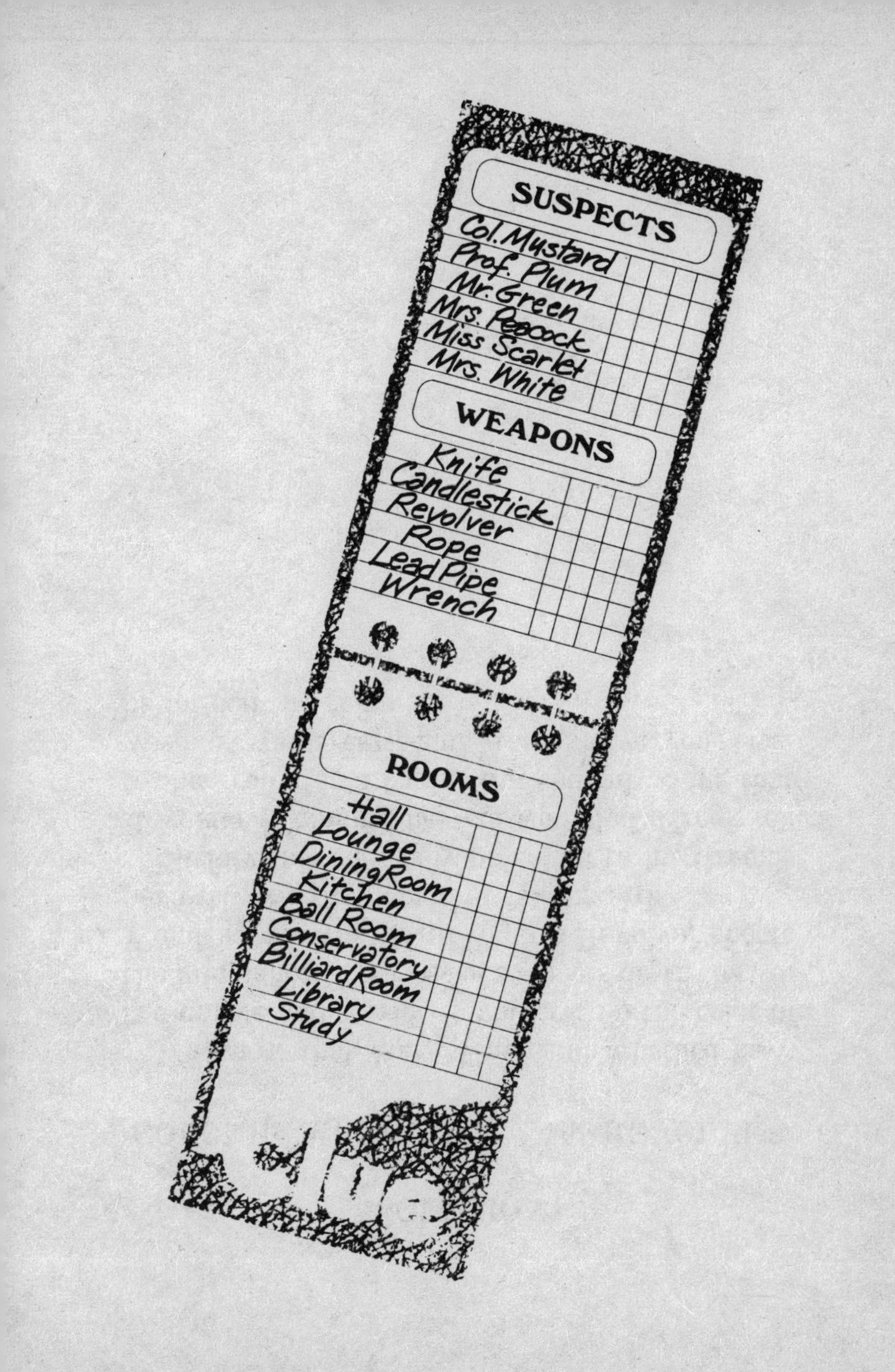
SUSPECTS
Col. Mustard
Prof. Plum
Mr. Green
Mrs. Peacock
Miss Scarlet
Mrs. White
WEAPONS
Knife
Candlestick
Revolver
Rope
Lead Pipe
Wrench
ROOMS
Hall
Lounge
Dining Room
Kitchen
Ball Room
Conservatory
Billiard Room
Library
Study
clue

SOLUTION

COLONEL MUSTARD with the REVOLVER

We know that Mrs. White and Mustard have the purple and scarlet Revolvers. So the color of the gun narrows our list of suspects down to two. We also know that Mrs. White's Revolver shoots perfectly. So the murderer is Mustard.

Luckily, his shot only managed to hit Green's Revolver. Thinking he was wounded, Green fell to the ground in a fright. But the only thing that was hurt was Green's aim. And like everyone else, he missed the rhino.

9
A Purple Belt in Karate

IN THE BILLIARD ROOM, MR. BODDY was pacing up and down, his face a mask of tension.

"Please take off that silly mask," Mrs. White told her boss. "It's making me nervous."

Mr. Boddy took off the plastic mask and tossed it on the pool table. But even without the mask, he still looked very worried. "How can I calm down?" he cried. "Tomorrow is Sunday, the big day. Just think. The First International Monopoly Tournament will be held right here at the Boddy mansion."

"It's very exciting," said Mrs. White. "You should feel proud." As Mr. Boddy paced toward her, she beamed proudly. As he paced away, she scowled with jealousy.

"But you know how tense these Monopoly tournaments can become," Mr. Boddy said. "There could be fighting."

"Oh, come on," said the maid. "Fighting? Among *your* guests?"

"Call me a worrywart," Boddy said. "But the

crime rate has risen so sharply these past few years . . ."

"Especially *inside* the mansion," muttered Mrs. White under her breath. Aloud, she said, "You'll just have to *watch* yourself." As she said it, she stole Mr. Boddy's watch.

Mr. Boddy started wringing his hands.

"Please stop wringing your hands," Mrs. White said. "You're driving me bats."

Mr. Boddy stopped wringing his hands.

"I thought I asked you to stop wringing," Mrs. White said.

"I did," said the puzzled host.

Mrs. White stood. "You're right. That wasn't your hands wringing. It was the doorbell ringing! Our first guest has arrived!"

Mrs. White ran from the room. Mr. Boddy ran after her, but he crashed into the lamp.

And then — a light bulb went on over his head. He sat down in a daze, but there was a smile on his face. "What a great idea!" he exclaimed proudly.

That afternoon at four . . .

That afternoon at four, Mr. Boddy's guests were all gathered in the Lounge. Everyone, including Mr. Boddy and Mrs. White, was wearing a kimono. Mr. Boddy, who was also wearing a lamp shade on his head, was addressing his guests.

"It was as if a light bulb went on over my head," he explained. "I asked myself how I could protect everyone from any possible crimes at tomorrow's tournament. Then it hit me like a lamp in the head. Self-defense! That's how we could all protect ourselves. And as luck would have it . . ."

Mr. Boddy turned to beam at Mrs. Peacock who beamed back. Mr. Boddy said, "We have one of the world's greatest self-defense experts staying with us in the mansion this weekend. Let's have a big hand for Mrs. Peacock!"

"Thank you, Mr. Boddy." Plump Mrs. Peacock stepped forward. She was wearing a blue kimono, along with her peacock-feather hat. She was also carrying a Lead Pipe. "I'd like to begin with a little demonstration. This is one of the most basic and most useful self-defense techniques," she said. "I call it the 'Stop It!' technique. Any volunteers?"

Professor Plum, who was wearing a purple kimono, raised his hand.

"Ah," Mrs. Peacock said, "Professor Plum."

"What, Mrs. Peacock?" Plum asked, lowering his hand.

Mrs. Peacock said sternly, "Come up here, Professor."

Professor Plum walked over to Mrs. Peacock.

"Now," said Peacock. "What I want you to do,

I want you to take this Lead Pipe, go to the other side of the room, and charge me at full speed. Got it?"

"Could you repeat the last part of the instructions?" asked Plum.

Mrs. Peacock looked annoyed. "All right. Which part?"

"The part after you said, 'Come up here, Professor.' "

Sighing, Mrs. Peacock repeated the instructions. Then she handed Plum the Lead Pipe. He marched to the edge of the room. Mrs. Peacock went into a defensive crouch. Everyone waited.

"Well?" Mrs. Peacock asked finally.

"Well what?" called the Professor.

Sighing even more loudly, Mrs. Peacock repeated the instructions a third time.

"Right," said Plum. He raised the Pipe over his head with both hands, shouted at the top of his lungs, and charged.

He was about to clonk Mrs. Peacock right on the head.

But just before he hit her, she yelled, "PROFESSOR PLUM! STOP IT!!"

Plum stopped, the Lead Pipe poised in mid-air.

"Drop the Pipe!" ordered Mrs. Peacock.

Plum dropped it.

"Good," said Mrs. Peacock.

Suddenly, the woman became a blue blur of

motion. She got the poor professor in a stranglehold with the Wrench.

"The 'Stop It!' technique works best with students in a class situation," she explained to the rest of the guests, still gripping the professor with the Wrench.

"Urgggggg," groaned Plum.

Mrs. Peacock continued to address the class. "Real-life criminals are rarely polite enough to take orders," she explained. "But if you happen to know that the criminal is polite, then this technique is just perfect."

"Ummmm," moaned Plum.

"What?" asked Mrs. Peacock. "Oh, sorry!"

Finally, she let the professor go. He fell over like a sack of plums. Mrs. Peacock took a little bow, and everyone applauded.

Mrs. Peacock helped Plum back to his feet. "Thank you, Professor," she said. "Keep up the good work and you'll soon earn yourself a purple belt."

"It will go nicely with my bruises," quipped Plum.

"All right," Mrs. Peacock said. "Let's pair off into small groups and work on the 'Stop It!' technique. And then I will go around and give you each some individual lessons."

Mrs. Peacock took Mr. Green aside first. She taught Green a judo throw, a karate chop, and a little pinch (Mrs. Peacock said little pinches hurt more than big ones).

Then Mrs. Peacock had Mrs White practice ducking, screaming for help, and karate chops. "Very good," Mrs. Peacock said. "There's just one more move I'd like to teach you. The Kung Fu Klobber."

"The Kung Fu Klobber?" the maid asked. "What's *that*?"

Mrs. Peacock didn't seem to be listening. She was looking past the maid toward the door. "Oh, my goodness," she breathed. "Why here's Kung Fu himself! He can demonstrate the move better than anyone."

Mrs. White turned toward the door. While she was turned, Mrs. Peacock *klobbered* her with all her might. Mrs. White fell to the floor and lay there like a dust rag. "And that," Mrs. Peacock told the fallen maid, "is the Kung Fu Klobber."

Then she went on with her individual lessons. Next she taught Miss Scarlet the little pinch, the karate chop, the judo throw, and screaming for help.

Mustard learned to call 9-1-1, the Kung Fu Klobber, and the judo throw.

Plum was only able to master screaming for help.

"Well," Boddy said, studying his bare wrist with a puzzled expression. "I think we're just about out of time. Let's all thank Mrs. Peacock."

The guests all applauded. Mrs. Peacock bowed.

"And don't forget to pay her," Mr. Boddy reminded everyone.

Mrs. Peacock held her hand out. "That's five dollars each."

The guests went to retrieve their purses and wallets. In a moment, everyone was back to pay their teacher. But —

As one of the guests was paying —

The guest dropped a roll of thousands on the floor.

Everyone saw the money except Mrs. Peacock.

Late that night . . .

Late that night, there was the sound of snoring in the Study. One of the guests was sleeping on the sofa. The room was pitch-black.

Except for the snoring, the rest of the mansion was quiet. But only for a moment. Because just then —

Creak.

Someone started *creak-creak-creaking* down the front stairs.

Whoever it was, was headed for —

The Study.

The guest in the Study snored on.

Even as the Study door creaked open.

Even as the other guest tiptoed into the dark room.

The thief reached into the pocket of the sleeping guest —

But just then —

The sleeping guest woke up with a start. "Thief!" gasped the guest.

The other guest just snarled.

And now the two guests began to fight in the dark room. It was a bitter struggle. Lamps fell with a crash. Furniture toppled with a bang. The two guests fought on, fighting for their lives.

In the course of the fight, the guest who'd been sleeping tried two self-defense techniques. They were techniques the guest had learned in that day's self-defense class: the judo throw and screaming.

Unfortunately, the attacking guest also tried some of Peacock's techniques from class. The attacker did the judo throw and followed it with a karate chop.

The karate chop was so powerful, it ended the fight.

Ended it once and for all.

WHO ATTACKED WHOM?

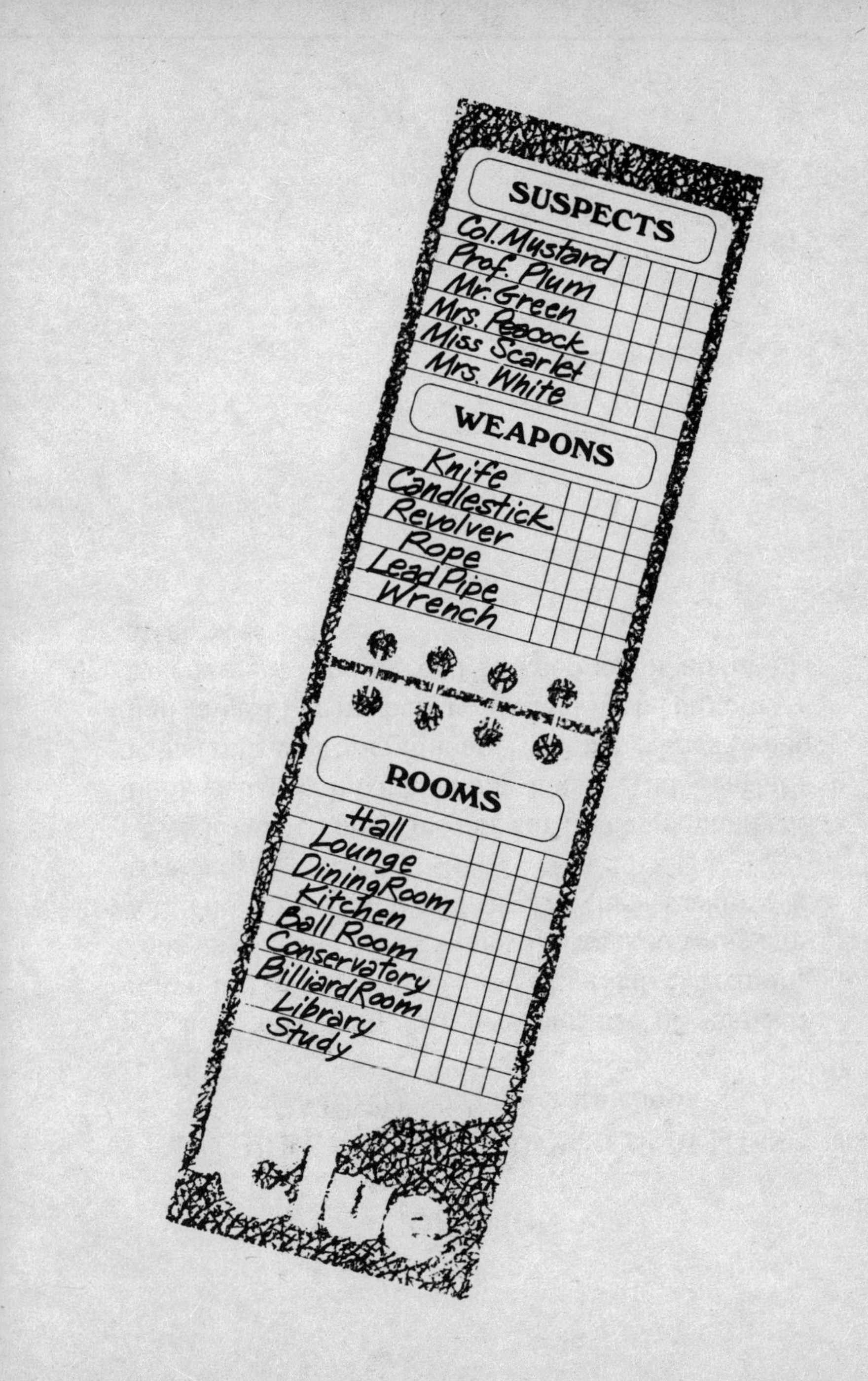
SUSPECTS
Col. Mustard
Prof. Plum
Mr. Green
Mrs. Peacock
Miss Scarlet
Mrs. White
WEAPONS
Knife
Candlestick
Revolver
Rope
Lead Pipe
Wrench
ROOMS
Hall
Lounge
Dining Room
Kitchen
Ball Room
Conservatory
Billiard Room
Library
Study

SOLUTION

MR. GREEN in the STUDY attacked MISS SCARLET with a karate chop.

The judo throw narrows our list of suspects down to Green, Scarlet, and Mustard. Screaming tells us that the guest who was attacked was Scarlet. The karate chop tells us that the attacker was Green.

As it turned out, Green's karate chop ended the fight because he'd hurt his hand. And Scarlet's roll of bills was only Monopoly money. Since Green had caught her preparing to cheat in the next day's tournament, she agreed to keep silent about his attempted robbery.

10
Mr. Boddy's Funeral

RIGHT SMACK IN THE MIDDLE OF BODdy's Ball Room sat a large black casket. It was an awful and gloomy sight.

What an awful and gloomy sight, thought Mrs. Peacock. All dressed in black, she was sitting on the love seat and facing the closed coffin. She was sniffling into a peacock-blue handkerchief. "Poor Mr. Boddy," she whimpered. "To die so young — how impolite!"

In her other hand she held a letter written on black stationery. When she glanced at the letter, she sniffled harder.

Then she heard someone singing. She froze, staring at the Ball Room door. The door flew open.

"Oh, what a happy day!" sang Professor Plum as he danced into the room. He was wearing a bright purple suit and a corsage of purple flowers.

"Professor Plum!" cried Mrs. Peacock, sitting up straight. "How dare you sing at a time like this?!"

Plum glanced at his watch. "Ten of two?"

"No, fool! It's Mr. Boddy's funeral!"

A light seemed to dawn in the Professor's eyes. He reached into the pocket of his purple vest and pulled out a black envelope. He glanced at what was printed there.

REGINALD BODDY'S FUNERAL
SUNDAY AT 2:00 P.M. IN THE BALL ROOM
PLEASE ATTEND

Plum slapped his forehead. "I knew there was a reason I came to the mansion today!"

The sound of a woman weeping at the door made Plum turn his head toward the piano. Then he realized his mistake and looked to the door.

Miss Scarlet, wearing all black, swept into the room. Behind her veil, she was crying softly.

"Miss Scarlet!" Plum said with surprise. "I know what *I'm* doing here, but what's *your* excuse?"

"She's here for the funeral just like you, of course," Mrs. Peacock snapped.

"Such a shame," Miss Scarlet said. "Such a terrible shame."

"Oh, yes," agreed Mrs. Peacock, sniffling louder.

But then Miss Scarlet smiled. "Well," she said, "at least we can be grateful about the will."

"Oh! How uncouth!" gasped Mrs. Peacock.

"What will?" asked Plum.

Miss Scarlet sighed. Then she reminded the Professor what was going on.

Two weeks ago, Mr. Boddy had deleted the names of his five guests and his maid from his will. He said he was fed up with people trying to murder him.

That was two weeks ago. Last week, Mr. Boddy had accepted everyone's sincere promise that they would never try to murder him again. The trusting Mr. Boddy had written his friends' names back into his will.

"Just think, if he had died before he put our names back in his will," Miss Scarlet said, "we would have been left without a penny. Now that would have been a *real* tragedy."

Gasping with outrage, Mrs. Peacock jumped to her feet. "*Really!*" she said. "How can you talk of money at a time like this?! How perfectly vulgar!" She glanced at the coffin. "Right in front of the body of Boddy."

"Believe me, he can't hear us," said Miss Scarlet. She started to dance Professor Plum around the Ball Room, singing, "We're rich, we're rich, we're rich!"

"Puhlease!" roared Mrs. Peacock. "Have you no manners whatsoever? Don't you know that money is — "

"Is what?" interrupted Mr. Green. He was standing in the doorway in a bright green suit.

He held up his funeral invitation. He'd had it laminated. "This is the best news I've gotten in a long time," he said. "I've already started spending my inheritance. On the way here, I bought myself this new green suit."

He spun around slowly, modeling his new outfit. "What do you think? Please be honest." Then he bared his teeth. "But if you don't like it, I'll step on your toesies!" He roared with mean laughter.

"Mr. Green! How dare you?"

It was Colonel Mustard, all dressed in black. He had just entered the Ball Room. He was glaring at Mr. Green, his eyepiece bobbing up and down in fury. "You can stand there laughing during poor Mr. Boddy's funeral?" The Colonel whipped out his own funeral invitation and slapped Mr. Green in the face with it. "I challenge you to a duel!"

"Please," cried Mrs. Peacock. "Fighting at a funeral is the height of rudeness. Mr. Green, apologize."

"Never!" barked Green.

"Fine," said Mustard. "It's your funeral."

"I thought it was Mr. Boddy's funeral," said a puzzled Plum.

Just then, Mustard yanked out the silver Wrench and waved it over his head. He moved slowly toward Mr. Green.

"You don't scare me," growled Green. "I've got something up my sleeve myself." Mr. Green pulled the Rope out of his sleeve and began lashing it at Mustard like a whip.

"Look at them! Dueling at a funeral!" cried Mrs. Peacock. "How coarse!" Just then, Green's Rope snicked Mrs. Peacock's peacock feather right in half. Her mouth fell open in speechless horror.

"Both of you — stop this at once!" screeched Mrs. White. She was standing in the doorway. She was dressed in her maid's black outfit, but she had switched her standard white hat for a black one. "Have you no decency?" she cried.

Mr. Green and Colonel Mustard stopped fighting and lowered their heads. "She's right," Mustard said. "We should be ashamed."

"We're the worst," agreed Green.

Then they started fighting again.

When Mrs. White saw the coffin, she started weeping. She tottered across the room and fell to her knees before the black box. Hugging the coffin, she cried, "My poor, poor boss." She paused to blow her nose into her invitation, then went back to weeping.

"She's upset that she won't have anyone to steal from," muttered Miss Scarlet.

Mrs. Peacock looked at her watch. "Two o'clock and still no Reverend. How horribly rude of him to be late!"

"Late for what?" asked Mr. Boddy, entering the room.

"MR. BODDY!!!!!!!!!!!!!!!!!!!!!!!!!!!!!!!!!!!!"

All the guests screamed in horror. Miss Scarlet fainted into the arms of Professor Plum. Then she fainted into the arms of Mr. Green.

"But — but — " Mrs. Peacock stammered.

"You're supposed to be — " gasped Miss Scarlet.

"Dead," finished Mr. Green.

"Dead?" Mr. Boddy asked, looking shocked.

"Wait a minute," Mustard said. "If you're here and alive, then who — " He turned and pointed to the coffin.

The guests all ran to the coffin and opened its thick, heavy lid.

The coffin was empty.

"How very odd," whispered Mrs. Peacock.

"I don't understand," Mr. Boddy said weakly.

Colonel Mustard slapped his host on the back. "Well, you see, Boddy old boy, we thought this was your funeral."

Boddy turned even paler. "My funeral?!"

By way of explanation, the guests whipped out the five black funeral invitations. "You see?" Miss Scarlet said.

Mr. Boddy's knees wobbled. Luckily, Professor Plum grabbed him and held him up. Then Plum forgot what he was doing and dropped Mr. Boddy in a heap on the floor.

"Don't bother getting up, Mr. Boddy," one of the guests said quietly.

Instantly, a hush fell over the room.

Because the guest had taken out a Knife.

"What is the meaning of this?" Boddy asked from the floor.

"Allow me to explain," the guest explained. "You see, *I* was the one who invited you all to Boddy's funeral."

"You!" cried Boddy and the other guests.

"I," the guest agreed. "And Boddy's funeral it will be!"

Then the guest raised the Knife high over Boddy's body.

"No — no!" screamed Boddy.

"No — no!" the other guests cried half heartedly.

"You won't get away with this," Boddy warned.

"But I will," the guest said. "That's the beauty of my plan."

"But there are witnesses," said Boddy, gesturing around the room.

"Yes, Mr. Boddy," the guest with the Knife said. "These people will all be witnesses. But since we're all named in your will, we all share an equal motive for killing you." The guest with the Knife faced the other guests. "The police won't believe you weren't part of this, I can assure you. That's why I invited you all here. This way I can be sure you'll all keep quiet. And I know *you* will keep quiet, Mr. Boddy."

Without further ado, the guest murdered poor Boddy.

WHO KILLED BODDY?

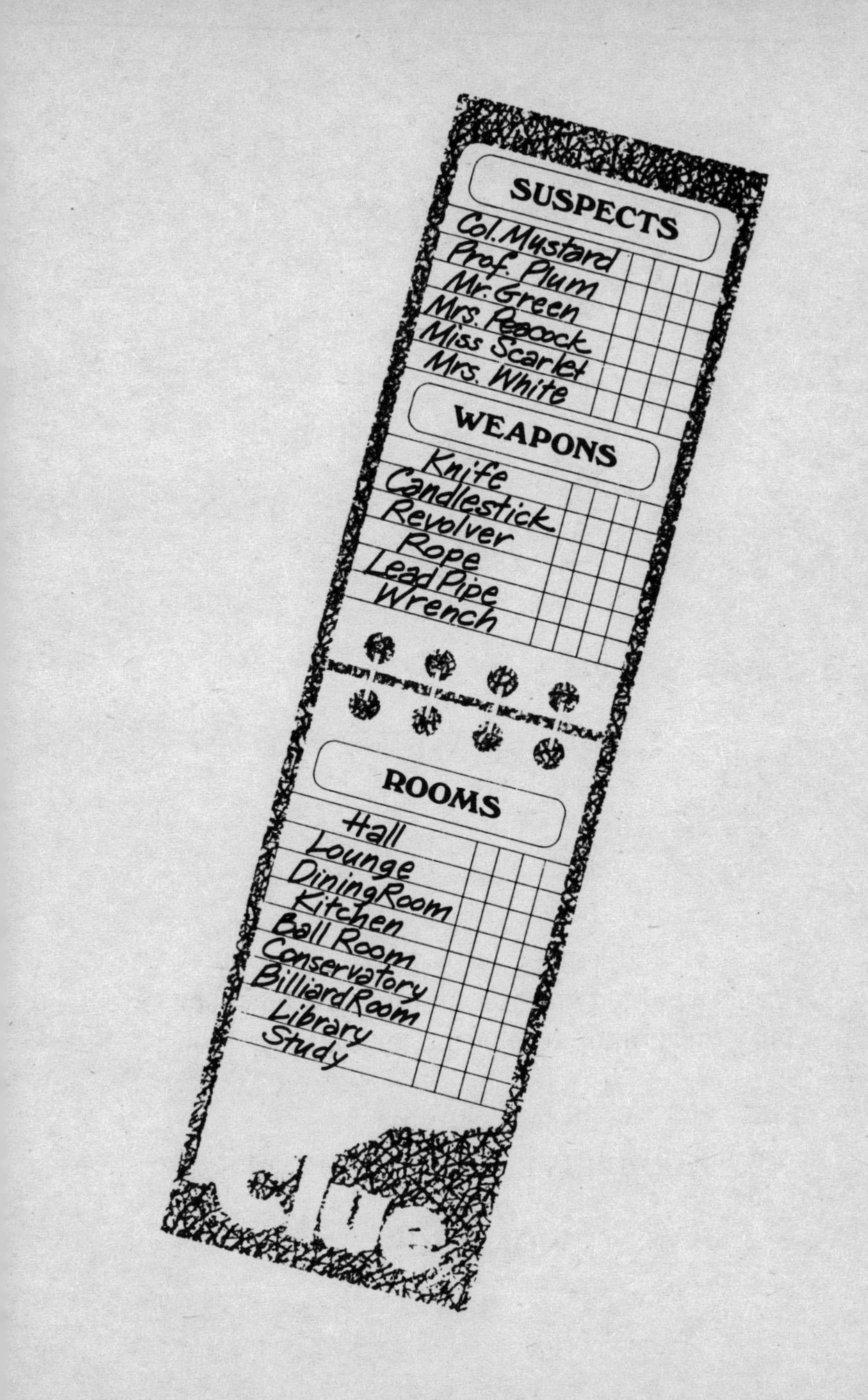
SUSPECTS
Col. Mustard
Prof. Plum
Mr. Green
Mrs. Peacock
Miss Scarlet
Mrs. White
WEAPONS
Knife
Candlestick
Revolver
Rope
Lead Pipe
Wrench
ROOMS
Hall
Lounge
Dining Room
Kitchen
Ball Room
Conservatory
Billiard Room
Library
Study

SOLUTION

MISS SCARLET in the BALL ROOM with
the KNIFE

She's the only one without an invitation. That's because she sent the invitations herself.